Gladly Missed

by

S Ben Hawksworth

Grosvenor House
Publishing Limited

This book is published by
Grosvenor House Publishing Ltd
Link House
140 The Broadway, Tolworth, Surrey, KT6 7HT.
www.grosvenorhousepublishing.co.uk

This book is a work of fiction. Any resemblance to
people or events, past or present, is purely coincidental.

A CIP record for this book
is available from the British Library

Paperback ISBN 978-1-83615-326-9

Geoffrey Hawksworth
9.1.1948 – 23.1.1948

To the older brother I never knew.
You only stayed for a couple of weeks,
but your short visit caused ripples that
spread through subsequent generations.
Sorry I didn't get to meet you, our kid.

Other books by
S Ben Hawksworth

Silly Beggars

Claiming the Blame

Genteel Anarchists

CHAPTER ONE

It is a commonly held misconception that graveyards are designed for the dead. True, the graves contain the dead, but the graveyard is solely for the living. The neat, often over-manicured plots within which the graves are set are purely there for those who visit. It is a place for some to sit quietly and talk to an unhearing headstone in an attempt to find some solace in communing with a departed friend or relative. For others, it is a place to sit in silence, perhaps reflecting on their own mortality.

No such morbid thoughts occupied the minds of Georgia and Steve as they sat together on one of the wooden benches that were to be found in the graveyard of Saint Augustine's. It was a quiet place where they could spend a few private moments together. The couple had met during their first week at university when they had ventured to the Freshers Ball, where Steve had been immediately impressed by Georgia and decided that he should engineer a situation where he could get to know her better. He needn't have bothered with his planning because Georgia had already decided that he was the one, out of the hundreds of young men at the dance, that she was going to claim as hers. Like many men before him, he had naively assumed that it was they who made such important decisions.

The two young students soon found that they got on extremely well, and for the rest of their university life, they were regarded by their friends as an inseparable couple around the campus. They minimised the agony of separation during the vacations by occasionally visiting each other's homes for extended weekend breaks. Steve's parents, and particularly his mother with her devout Baptist upbringing, made it quite clear that whatever Steve might get up to at university, while Georgia was at their house, the sleeping arrangements did not permit the couple to share a bed. Initially, Georgia's mother had adopted the same philosophy, but she very soon realised that the young couple shared a stable relationship and agreed to Georgia's suggestion that the couple should be able to spend some time in the flat above her florist shop. Thus it was that Georgia and Steve preferred to stay in her home village of Hartbridge over the holidays, where they occupied the small flat above the shop and made a little extra money by helping out in the family business.

When their respective courses drew to a close, Steve and Georgia had set about the task of finding employment for themselves, but this had proved more difficult than they expected. They had both been encouraged by their families to go to university in the expectation that they would walk out at the end and step straight into lucrative careers. The reality was somewhat different, and as they sat in the churchyard that evening, neither of them had received any offers of employment despite sending off dozens of applications. That was not going to spoil their evening as he sat with a loving arm over her shoulders, and they shared lengthy kisses from time to time. Enjoying the late afternoon sun, they periodically looked over at a young workman who was carefully clipping the grass around one of the older graves in the cemetery. It was a classic bucolic setting. This rural idyll could have been the inspiration for Gray's Elegy. It all seemed so perfect to the young lovers as they sat and discussed their future together while the groundsman finished his work for the day before coming over to take a seat on the bench next to them.

Most young couples would have slightly resented this intrusion into their romantic moment, but they knew that this was Stan and he was a bit 'different'.

"Evening, Georgia. Evening, Steve," he announced in a rather formal manner in a voice that was devoid of any marked tonal variation.

"Hi, Stan," replied Georgia. "I see you've been busy again. You certainly keep this place looking beautiful."

"Oh yes," he replied, casting a lengthy gaze around the deserted churchyard before continuing, "I have to keep it nice for my friends."

Steve looked up at this point, slightly startled to hear this reference to Stan's 'friends' and concerned for a moment that he regarded the occupants of the graves as real people. It was known within the village that Stan had certain problems after a tragic accident some years previously, so perhaps he was confused on the issue.

"They'll be coming to see me soon. If you stay very quiet, they will come over to see us."

The three occupants of the bench sat in silence for a while, and then two squirrels appeared from the bushes by one of the large trees and ran over and stood beside Stan. Taking off his heavy working gloves, he carefully took two nuts out of his overall pocket and threw them gently in the direction of the visitors who each took one and scuttled off back towards the safety of the bushes. This procedure was repeated several times until the more adventurous of the two was eventually content to take a nut from Stan's outstretched hand. The young couple were impressed by the gentle way Stan treated his friends. It seemed strange that a man of his impressive stature could be so gentle. He was over six foot six inches tall and had an imposing physique, making him have the general appearance of a night club bouncer rather than part-time gravedigger and groundsman.

It was only when he walked that the discerning eye could have noticed that he tended to display an almost imperceptible limp. The only other obvious effect of his accident was his speech; while it was perfectly clear, it was slightly slow and invariably delivered in a flat monotone, which generally conveyed little emotion.

"My other friends are a bit scared of people, so they don't like to get close unless I'm on my own," he said, gesturing towards a group of rooks in a tree just beyond the graveyard wall, "and some of them only come at regular times when they know I'm having my lunch. They know I always try to bring them something."

After this last remark, he bid goodbye to the young couple, put his gloves on again, gathered his tools in his barrow and headed towards his shed in the corner of the churchyard.

"So, what exactly did happen to Stan?" queried Steve. "It was before I ever visited Hartbridge."

"I was still at school myself, but it was a big issue in the local paper and a major talking point around here. Stan was a few years older than me, but he had been to the same secondary school as I had. He had quite a reputation and was often held up as a role model when I was at school. We were repeatedly told how he had been a brilliant scholar and gone off to Oxford University. We never had any Oxbridge entrants before Stan. As well as that, he was quite a local celebrity in other areas; he played for the village football team, captained the cricket team, and he had a good degree. We had a school band that played the local circuit, and Stan was the lead singer in that as well. You might have thought that the local boys would have hated him for being so perfect, but they didn't. He was always modest and never showed any sign of being conceited about any of his talents. He always seemed to be friendly with everybody. On top of that, he was gorgeous, and there's no wonder that a lot of the older girls were mad keen on him, but he ended up going out with a young woman who was training at the army camp down the road in Callerthorpe. I think her name was Judy.

"One night there was a dance at the Callerthorpe cricket club, but Judy was on duty, so Stan reluctantly went on his own. It went on rather late, and Stan, being the responsible individual he always was, opted to walk home rather than risk driving as he'd had a few pints. He was almost back in the village and just walking on the bridge over the river when he was hit by a car. Poor old Stan was knocked clean over the parapet of the bridge and was lucky not to land in the water. The police later revealed that if he had been hit while walking over the central arch, he would have fallen into the river and drowned. He apparently landed half in the water, but his head was on the grass bank, and so he survived, but only just. The driver didn't bother to stop, and it was a sheer fluke that a fisherman found Stan very early the next morning and alerted the emergency services. He was flown by helicopter to a specialist hospital thirty miles away, and they put him into an induced coma. He was in the hospital for nearly a year with several operations and then a range of therapies which went on for months before he was able to come home. He's very lucky to be alive."

"So, did they ever find the driver who ran him down?"

"Eventually, but it took some time. It turns out that a local guy, Andy Cordwell, had reported his car stolen the morning after the incident, and the police were naturally suspicious of this convenient theft. Our local bobby, Constable-thick-as-a-brick Danny Bright, came into the pub and bragged about how he had solved the case, and he was sure that Andy Cordwell would be sent down for a long time. I went to school with Danny; he was never the most intelligent lad in the class, and he was known as Daft Danny then. They found the car abandoned some miles away and matched some of the headlight glass with some of the bits stuck to Stan's trousers. Things obviously looked bleak for Andy, who had no alibi for the time of the accident, but then Kirsty Allerton, a local girl, came up with some interesting evidence which she relayed to the local police. I knew Kirsty vaguely, and she had a deserved reputation for being a bit of a fun-loving individual who was very popular with the boys. Kirsty was a girl that Mrs Holland from the post office would describe as being 'no better than she ought to be'.

"Anyway, Kirsty had attracted the attention of a local lad called Brad Carter, a general trouble-causer in the village. Brad had offered to take her out for dinner at a local pub as he was keen to show off 'his' new car to her, and no doubt he expected he would benefit from this act of generosity when Kirsty would show her appreciation at the end of the evening. During their time at The Black Swan, he'd consumed a lot of beer and was very annoyed when she rejected his romantic advances and wouldn't go for a ride with him. She told the police that she'd made it abundantly clear that she was not going to spend any time in some secluded lane with him, particularly as the 'dinner' he had promised amounted to a pork pie and several large gins. As I said, Kirsty was a girl who liked to have a good time, and Brad, in his beer-driven state, assumed he was onto a good thing. Kirsty was known for being free with her favours, but she had her standards, and Brad fell far short of them in his state at the time. He lost his temper and drove off in a completely reckless manner, almost hitting the gatepost of the pub car park.

"It turns out that Brad, who had not been in the area long, had stolen the car just to impress the girl. The police were able to find DNA evidence to show he had been in it. Apparently, the idiot hadn't been wearing his seatbelt, and in a subsequent crash into a wall that night, he had split his head open. There was blood all over the interior of the car and he needed stitches. It left him with a nasty scar across his forehead, but he got no sympathy from anyone around here. The evidence against him was overwhelming and, in the end, he confessed. He claimed that he had not been aware that he'd hit anybody and thought it might have been a badger he had hit. Some badger!"

"I hope they threw the book at him."

"The judge was limited as to what he could do under the sentencing guidelines but, having listened to an extensive list of Brad's previous driving offences, gave him a five-year prison sentence and a two-year driving ban, after which he would have to retake his test. In his summing up, the judge made it very clear that he would have liked to impose a longer sentence on the accused, whom he formally addressed as Bradley Bartholomew Carter, but he was not permitted to do so. Brad probably only did three and a half years and will have been out for a few years now, but Stan's sentence continues. Even his girlfriend, Judy, didn't stick around. To be fair to her, they hadn't been together long, and it was never intended to be a long-term thing. Her army posting abroad made it difficult, but it was just one more disappointment for Stan, along with the realisation that his sporting days are over."

"So, he spends his time looking after the churchyard?"

"Yes. He's a big, strong chap, as you can see, and he works as an informal sexton at the church here. He's proven to be very good at grave digging, but fortunately that's not a full-time job. The villagers are generally very supportive of him, and he does all sorts of odd jobs, as and when needed."

"I've seen him around the village, but being relatively new here, I didn't know about his history," added Steve.

"It's rather a tragic story. Stan's mum died when he was in hospital, and the identity of his father was never known. There were rumours, as there always are in a small community, but nobody was sure who the father was. When Stan did eventually come out of hospital, he was taken in by his gran, old Martha Turner, and he still lives with her."

"It's a good job he had someone to support him."

"Yes, I suppose so, but old Mrs Turner isn't the doting grandmother that one might have assumed she is and indeed claims to be. Stan has to give the vast majority of any small amounts of money he receives to her and, in return, she calls him all sorts of names in her gossip within the village. She will declare how lucky he is to be under her roof as his 'good-for-nothing father' has never done anything to share the costs. Pretty much everyone in the village knows how she exploits him. He has a pokey little room, and she encourages him to be out of the house as much as possible so he isn't 'under her feet all day'. As a result, he sometimes spends hours wandering around the village. He can't afford to go to the pub, except for the odd half of bitter, and in cold weather he goes up to the churchyard and settles himself in his hut where he has a little oil stove. He will sometimes stay there until he feels it's a reasonable time to go home. Some of the villagers try to help a bit by inviting him in for the odd meal or cup of coffee, and locals at the pub will sometimes include him in a round, even when they know he can't afford to buy a drink in return. The truth is that it's the villagers who make his life a little more bearable, not his money-grabbing gran."

The couple sat in silence for a while, enjoying the tranquillity of the setting. It was a warm evening, but Steve couldn't help but think about Stan having to spend a lot of time outside or in his shed during the colder months. Steve looked fondly at Georgia as she sat beside him looking out over the quiet churchyard, and he couldn't help but appreciate how lucky he was. He was living with the woman he loved, and they had both just finished university with degrees that they had every right to expect would eventually lead them into good careers. In short, life was good for them, while Stan's future had been so cruelly blighted; his academic prowess and his sporting skills were now all part of a past that he couldn't remember, and he had lost his girlfriend along the way as well. He had no recollection of what she had looked like or anything about their previous relationship, but had heard people talk about her and this had created a false memory of someone he knew he had been rather fond of. There was also the inescapable irony that Stan had done the right thing and chosen not to drive after drinking that night, and that is why he had been walking over the bridge when he did. The bright and happy future that he deserved had been taken from him by the selfish, reckless actions of a drunk who only got a few short years in prison. Steve felt a justifiable sense of the unfairness that life presents some people and a futile anger at the fact that there was nothing that he could do about it.

"It just occurred to me," reflected Georgia. "Stan must have been little more than our age when he was knocked down. It makes me appreciate how much he lost. It's all rather depressing. Let's not dwell on it; why don't we wander down to the Trout after dinner? I'm sure our budget can extend to a couple of glasses of wine?"

The Trout Inn was the village pub and had been re-named as such in the late twentieth century, having previously been called The Lemont Arms after some local aristocratic family who had owned large swathes of land in the area. The new name was a reference to the fact that the pub sat on the banks of the local river with an extensive lawned area that served as a beer garden to the rear that ran down to the water's edge.

Beyond the river was a large nature reserve, which served as a beautiful backdrop to the view from the pub. Nobody could remember any trout being taken from that stretch of river for decades, but the romantic suggestion that it could contain such fish led to the new name for the pub.

The Trout Inn was a relatively large building with a spacious car park to the front. It had been envisaged and even promoted as the archetypal country pub where people from the local towns could spend a couple of hours after work or drive down on a weekend in the summer to sit outside in the garden with its extensive views out over the river. The enforcement of drink-driving laws had hit the pub a lot, and it was no longer the magnet for visitors who drove there. Most of the time, it got by on the patronage of the locals and by providing meals. When Steve and Georgia arrived there that evening the pub was far from full and most of the clients had apparently chosen to sit outside rather than stay in the lounge bar. As the couple walked in, they were greeted by Monica, the barmaid.

"Hello, my lovelies, and what can I get you this evening?"

"Two glasses of red, please, Monica. It seems particularly quiet in here tonight. I was expecting to see Colin and young Mark in," said Georgia.

"They'll be in soon. There was some sort of dramatic performance at Mark's day centre, and Colin was going to go along to show his support. I'm sure that Mark won't want to miss his Vesper Martini."

"Vesper Martini?" queried Steve. "That's a bit sophisticated for the Trout."

"It's Mark's alter ego, James Bond; he won't drink anything else. We can cope with his drink of choice, but his outrageous flirting can raise a few eyebrows on those who don't know him," said Monica.

"You must excuse my friend's obvious confusion," explained Georgia. "He's only just got back from university and, apart from the occasional short visits over the last couple of years, he's relatively new to the area and has yet to have the pleasure of getting to know Mark and his eccentric ways."

It was at this point that two newcomers approached the bar. One was an elderly man, and the other was a young man who obviously had Down syndrome. The latter strode up to the bar purposefully and addressed Monica.

"A Vesper Martini, please, beautiful lady, and a pint for Dad."

Monica dutifully pulled a pint for the older visitor, and then, having selected a bottle from the fridge, she poured some of it into a champagne coupe. She added a splash of soda water before spearing a cocktail cherry and placing it gracefully in the drink.

"There you are, Mark," said the barmaid, placing his drink on the bar.

"Thank you, my sweetheart darling," came the reply, and then after taking a sip, he continued, "Exquisite!" Taking his drink and leaving his father to pay, he moved over to one of the many little tables and sat down to observe what was going on in the bar, as any good secret agent would. Meanwhile, his father stood at the bar with his pint.

"Hi Colin, I gather you've been at the day centre with Mark for some kind of performance this afternoon," commented Georgia.

"Yes, I like to show my support. The trainees have a choir. They don't claim to be very good, but they enjoy singing, and afterwards we have coffee and cakes. Mark loves that part so he can charm all his lady friends. He sees himself as some sort of lothario, but if any of them responded to his overtures, he'd run a mile. I guess that, deep down, he isn't cut out to be James

Bond. His main reason for attending the socials is so that he can meet up with his girlfriend, Celia. She puts up with his extravagant flirting because she knows that she is the only girl he's really interested in."

"So I'm not the only girl in his life?" queried Georgia. "I must admit that his attempts at serenading women could do with polishing up a bit. I can't remember how often I've been regaled with his romantic vocalisations, which are usually restricted to, *'Beautiful lady, my sweetheart, won't you run away with me?'* The sentiments are clear, but the tune leaves much to be desired."

"Does he always drink those flash drinks?" asked Steve. "They must cost a fortune."

"They are Mark specials," explained Monica. "We mix up a bottle with apple juice, a dash of lemon juice and a couple of drops of angostura bitters. We add a squirt of soda water before serving and then a cherry on a stick. Relatively cheap and non-alcoholic. God knows how he might respond if he ever went into a bar and was served with the real thing."

Colin walked over to join his son, and they sat together chatting for a while.

"That's Colin Foreman and his son Mark," explained Georgia as she continued the informal induction of her boyfriend into village life. "Colin's wife, Jackie, died a couple of years ago, so he looks after Mark on his own now. Mark is a treasure and extremely sociable. He often comes in here on his own to meet up with friends, and in his case, his 'friends' are anyone he meets. He is permanently happy and sees himself as a comedian, telling awful jokes and often forgetting the punchlines. His view of life is ludicrously positive, so his glass is not just half full but positively brimming over. Colin is obviously getting on a bit and knows that he isn't going to live forever, so he's been trying to find some type of sheltered housing for his son."

"Is there anything you don't know about this place?" asked Steve.

"As you know, I lived here until I went off to university and came back during most holidays, and it is only a small community. Take Mrs Simpson over there," she said while discreetly nodding to an elderly lady. "She's the old pharmacist who used to work in the chemist's shop. As kids, we used to call her 'Potions Pamela' because of the way she used to dispense prescriptions, but not before explaining the possible side effects of the drugs in lurid details. We were all a bit scared of her, and there were completely unfounded rumours that she was some kind of witch. You know what children can be like."

When he found an opportunity to discreetly observe the former potions-vendor, Steve was surprised to see a smartly dressed elderly lady sitting on one of the benches down the side of the room with a small dog sitting beside her. As he watched, he saw how Mrs Simpson was carefully taking individual polo mints from her handbag and feeding them to her little companion, who sat attentively by her side. The dog was one of those indefinable balls of fur whose role in life was to act purely as companion rather than having any specific canine uses.

"Watch what happens in a moment," said Georgia in a hushed whisper. "Each time they come in, Mrs Simpson has a roll of mints in her handbag, which she systematically feeds to her little friend throughout their stay. When little Snoopy knows the mints have all gone, he will stop pestering her."

"That's not unusual," observed Steve. "My mum's dog would stop begging for crisps once he saw the bag was empty."

"Yes, but Snoopy can't see when the mints have all gone. He just seems to have some in-built mechanism, like counting, to know when he's had his allocation of mints. If Mrs Simpson pretends they've all gone, Snoopy doesn't believe her."

"There are some weird goings-on here in Hartbridge, and that's no mistake," commented Steve, before adding, "Why don't we grab another drink and take them into the garden?"

As the couple approached the back door to the lawn, they almost bumped into a tall man who was entering the pub. He graciously stepped back and let the young couple through. They thanked him and made their way to one of the picnic benches not far from the back of the pub, where they could look out in the fading evening light down the extensive lawn to the river and the reed beds beyond.

"That was Colonel Mike Colly we nearly bumped into in the doorway," explained Georgia. "Nobody is quite sure if he is an ex-colonel, but he is generally known as such. He's a bit of a mystery figure; some say he was in the Special Forces, but all we do know is that, latterly, he was stationed at Callerthorpe training camp, and it was suggested that he was giving specialised training in self-defence. As I say, he's a bit of an enigma, and the local rumour mill suggests he might have been Stan's father, but at some time over the years, the local gossips have suggested every male in the village of an appropriate age might have filled that role, even my own father. Mike never talks about his military experiences, and he's not the kind of guy you might want to upset by probing too deeply. He's really a very nice chap, though; he enjoys a quiet life, and his private passion is beekeeping; he has a number of bee hives he keeps down by the river and sells particularly good honey to his friends."

The young couple sat for some time before finishing their drinks and walking down to the banks of the river, where they stood for a while before Georgia announced, "The path along the riverbank goes along to the bridge where Stan had his accident," she said, pointing to what was little more than a worn track leading off into the descending darkness.

"Are you suggesting we might have a stroll down there in the moonlight?" he asked as he took her in his arms and kissed her.

"I am not," she said firmly. "For a start, there is precious little moonlight, and secondly, that path is a bit uneven in places, and I, for one, do not wish to have a late-night swim. The river can be dangerous at the best of times, and taking a plunge late at night after a couple of drinks might be seen as a bit of a risk."

"OK, scaredy cat," he teased her, "I guess you're right. We'd better take our glasses back to the bar and head off home."

The pub had filled up a little since they had left, and Georgia stopped a couple of times as she passed through with Steve, introducing him to some of the village residents along the way. When they eventually made it out of the front door, having noticed it was quite chilly, he took off his denim jacket and put it around her shoulders.

"Well, my darling, your place or mine?" he asked her seductively.

"You daft lump! As you are currently living at my place, I think the question is largely academic."

It was true that Steve had been staying in Georgia's flat since they came back from university. She had taken the small flat above her mother's florist shop, and she'd been pleased to take up the continuing offer of work in the shop and the option of staying in the flat while looking for a more permanent post. As Georgia's mother had given her a temporary place to live and work, and as the couple didn't want to be split up, Steve had taken a job in a large factory nearby which processed agricultural produce for freezing. His contract was due to start in two days' time when he was destined to play a small part in processing the pea harvest, so he was determined to have a mini holiday and to give himself a bit of time to find out more about the village. The entry to the flat was through the shop, and they were met by the scent of buckets of cut flowers and that indefinable smell of fresh greenery. As they moved through the shop, Steve was struck by the fact that the smell was infinitely preferable to the smell of cooking cabbage that always seemed to pervade the entrance hall to the cheap digs he'd had at university.

"Remember, Mum will be around early in the morning after she's been to the market to get some fresh stock, and I'll be starting work at nine, so don't expect to stay in bed all day," she told him.

"Shame, and I thought I would have a romantic holiday," he said with a sly grin.

"We could manage a short romantic break this evening, but I still have to be up early, and I have no intention of letting you lounge about in bed all day."

CHAPTER TWO

Georgia and Steve were just finishing their breakfasts the following morning when they heard the sound of the shop bell as her mother opened the front door. Steve immediately got up to assist in unpacking the flowers from the van and carrying them through to the shop.

He stood for a while looking at the smart little florist's van, which was decorated with the motif *'Fresh as a Daisy'*. It was this particular signage that had led him to assume that it was some kind of pun and that the owner was called Daisy. It was for this reason that he always addressed her by this name rather than her proper name, which was, in fact, Clara. It had become a shared joke, and he'd always got on very well with her.

"Thanks for that, love," said Clara as they finished unloading the day's flowers. "Now we've got time for a quick cuppa before I open up."

"My pleasure, Daisy," he said with a broad smile. "I'll just close the van up."

As he stood beside the van, he glanced over at the lychgate of the church, which was directly opposite; he remembered how Georgia had pointed out that the proximity of the church had meant a steady business in flower sales over the years. He looked out over the fields opposite and could just glimpse the odd stretch of the river. Beyond that, he knew there was an extensive area of low-lying marshy ground that had been declared a nature reserve, which he and Georgia had explored on a few occasions when he had spent time with her during their university years. It was a warm sunny morning, and he imagined for a moment that it was probably going to be a fine day for harvesting peas, but he had another day's holiday before that.

Up in the flat, Georgia had already prepared a pot of tea when her mother and Steve arrived.

"Hi Mum, how did you get on at the market?"

"Not bad, thanks, darling. I should have plenty of stock, but it's going to be fun keeping them cool in this weather. Rita knows all our regular little ploys for keeping the flowers fresh, and she should be along at nine. Did you enjoy your time at the Trout last night?"

"How did you know about that?" asked Steve.

"In this village, there are few secrets unless you go out of your way to hide them. I met Hannah Cordwell in the shop, and she mentioned she'd seen the pair of you," explained Clara, before adding, "I should be careful of her, Georgia; she seemed very keen on your Steve."

"Poor old Hannah, I don't think she's a great threat, but I know she has been very lonely since her husband, Andy, left her."

"Andy Cordwell?" queried Steve. "Isn't he the guy who was originally accused of running into Stan?"

"One and the same," replied Clara. "When that loud-mouthed feeble-minded local police officer announced, somewhat prematurely, that it was Andy in the car, there were some who believed him. Andy was soon vindicated, but he always resented the fact that he had been doubted, so he moved out of the village. That's the story that Hannah sticks to, but their marriage was generally known to be experiencing some difficulties, often more closely linked to her rumoured romantic dalliances rather than her husband's resentment of being falsely accused."

"This place is a cauldron of rumours," observed Steve with a smile. "I wonder what the locals have made of me so far."

"Give them time, darling. I've no doubt that the odd tongue has been wagging about the fact that we are living over the brush," commented Georgia.

"What? Living over a flower shop?"

"No," explained Clara. "And just to save my dear daughter's innocent blushes, I should explain. The term refers back to an old custom where a couple who couldn't get a church wedding would hold hands and step over a besom to show their commitment to one another; a sort of common law marriage."

"A besom?"

"Yes, a besom! It's the traditional name for the old-fashioned brush made of twigs tied around a long handle, the chosen mode of transport for witches," explained Georgia.

"Sounds a good idea. Perhaps we should get ourselves a besom?" he suggested.

"Not on your life, young man! If you want to indicate some commitment to my dear daughter, then I think you ought to get married," replied Clara before adding, "I could make a small fortune in flower sales."

Steve was reluctant to leave the two women in the shop, but he knew that Rita, the full-time assistant, would be arriving soon and he would only be getting in the way, so he chose to go off on his own to explore the village. He decided to check the village store out first if only to see the notorious Mrs Cordwell. He walked into the shop in what he hoped was a casual way and looked around. It was a small convenience store offering a wide range of goods and had an off-license section with a surprisingly large range of drinks. He wandered around a bit before selecting a chocolate bar from one of the displays which he took to the till. He was surprised to see that Mrs Cordwell was not serving as the individual who took his money was obviously in her late teens, at most.

"Morning," she greeted him in that almost robotic fashion that shop assistants can sometimes display, but then she looked up at him and, in a more animated voice, said, "Oh! Hello, you're Georgia's friend, aren't you? I'm Karen." There followed a brief outline as to how the young assistant had known Georgia for years, and their times at the local comprehensive school had briefly overlapped until Georgia had gone off to university. Fascinating as this conversation was, Steve was conscious of two other customers who were waiting in line to be served, so he was pleased when his own transaction was concluded by the ubiquitous instruction to 'have a nice day'.

Leaving the shop, he strolled slowly down the road, unwrapping his chocolate bar as he went. He passed the post office and sat on the bench by the bus stop. He had checked the timetable and knew he could get an early bus from there when he started work the following day. As he sat there in the warm sunshine, he became aware that he was being watched, less than surreptitiously, by a young police officer. This had to be the cerebrally-challenged Danny Bright. Steve surmised that he was watching to see if he intended to drop his chocolate wrapper on the floor, so when he finished his snack, he waved the wrapper in the air in the officer's direction before walking over and placing it in the bin, as had always been his intention. As he resumed his seat, the police officer walked over to speak to him.

"Morning, sir," said the officer in that strange, measured manner that was supposed to project an air of authority. "Are we new to the area, sir?"

Steve resisted the temptation to say that he was certainly a newcomer, but he wasn't sure whether the officer was local and simply replied, "Yes, I am indeed. I'm a friend of Georgia's."

"Glad to see you've done your bit to keep our village tidy, sir. Take care."

With this parting remark, the officer strolled off to perform whatever duties he might be called upon to try and perform. Steve managed not to laugh at the behaviour of the young man who was simply playing the part of a police officer. His antics were somewhere between the Keystone Cops and a pantomime figure. All his efforts to make himself look mature only made him look even less likely to command respect. Steve mused on the fact that some police officers do look younger these days, but Danny Bright looked as if he ought to still be in short trousers.

Steve sat for a while, looking at the village recreation ground on the opposite side of the road. In one corner of the field, there was a collection of pieces of playground apparatus, and in the middle of the wide expanse of grass was an area that had been roped off to protect what he knew to be the village cricket square. On his first afternoon of living in the village, he had walked past there with Georgia and had persuaded her to stop for a few minutes to watch a match being played out. It had seemed like the quintessential English village scene, and he had enjoyed leaning casually against the stone wall surrounding the park in the warm sunshine. In some inexplicable way, it had struck him that this was a special moment. There he was with the girl he intended to spend the rest of his life with. The moment took on a timeless quality, and he had even forgotten the cricket as he gently squeezed her hand. This apparently absent-minded gesture had meant so much to him. Georgia had obviously not appreciated the intensity of the moment, but he had filed it away among the experiences he knew he would always remember as their lives unfolded together.

Compared to the levels he had experienced playing for the university team, the standard of play had not been great, but the participants were obviously having a good time. He smiled as the memory of the day came back, and once again he experienced that feeling of contentment. His mind returned to Georgia's comment about Stan having been about their age when his life had been so dramatically altered by the accident. This was the ground where Stan would previously have led out the village team proudly. That was something else that had cruelly been snatched from him. The ground was the stereotypical English village centre with the broad field running down to the river. There was a pavilion, which was apparently an old wooden army hut that had been painted white, and two sight screens. All in all, it was a pretty sophisticated setup for a small village and suggested that the game was taken very seriously. It had occurred to him at the time that many shots must have resulted in the ball being lost to the murky water or, in the case of a very fine stroke, to the reed beds on the opposite bank.

He looked up and down the main street and suddenly realised that he had a day before him but little to fill it with. The pub might otherwise have been an attractive option, but he didn't like drinking on his own and was not one for drinking during the day. Apart from that, he recognised that he was, as yet, unemployed and could not afford to drop into the pub every time he was at a loose end. The small amount that he and Georgia had scraped together from their respective bar work as students would not support such extravagant living, and he wasn't going to live off the income she derived from working in the shop. He walked back and crossed over the road to the pub and noticed that there was a public footpath just before it that presumably ran down to the river and decided to explore that. He took the path that sloped gently down towards the water, and at that point, he followed the track that passed along the bottom of the pub's beer garden and headed in the direction Georgia had said would go to the bridge. He realised that she had been right to be cautious about the path as it ran perilously close to the river in places. It would certainly have been difficult to navigate it in the dark the previous evening. As he approached the bridge, he saw a collection of beehives set back from the river bank. He observed the occasional bee flying to and from them, their soothing drone invading the quiet of the morning and contributing to his general feeling of contentment. He assumed that they must be the hives belonging to the mysterious Colonel Mike Colly.

Steve was in no hurry, but even at his strolling pace, it took him less than five minutes to get to the bridge. He walked out over the central arch and gazed back in the direction of the pub. Because of the bend in the river, all but the roof of the pub was obscured, but looking back over the bridge, he had a clear view of the church. The day was heating up now, and he became a bit concerned at being out on the bridge in the hot sun. The water looked cool and inviting as he leant over the parapet and looked straight down into it, but he knew that it was quite fast flowing and there were beds of concealed weeds that could prove dangerous to an unwary swimmer. He peered down at the water as it rushed off in the direction of the pub, but then, he straightened up, and turning away from the mesmerising sight of the river, he headed back towards the church. Entering the churchyard through a small gate at the back, he walked up to the building to find somewhere to sit out of the sun. No sooner had he sat down than he heard a familiar voice.

"It's a lovely day but too hot for digging." The clear monotone voice was that of Stan, who was walking past with his barrow and a collection of grass-cutting implements.

"You're right, Stan. It's a scorcher."

"I saw you on the bridge. I don't go down there much. Too dangerous. Do you want a cup of tea?" Stan's mind flitted from one idea to the next; as he thought of something, he said it. He had no sophisticated filters, and that was part of his charm.

"As a matter of fact, Stan, I was just thinking that I could do with a drink. I'm parched."

Stan walked off slowly, pushing his barrow and assorted tools, and Steve followed him towards his shed. Having parked up his barrow and taken off his gloves, Stan unlocked the shed's twin doors and propped them open to let the daylight in.

"Come in and sit down. I'll put the kettle on."

Steve felt almost honoured to be invited into this special part of Stan's world. The shed had a tap in one corner and a small table which held a washing-up bowl and a small Calor gas ring. There was an old armchair and a stool which Steve chose to sit on in deference to the owner of the 'home'. The unmistakable smell of pine cladding and dried grass cuttings filled the air and reminded Steve of his days as a child in his grandfather's shed. There was no window to open, and it was quite warm in the current weather, but he imagined it would be pretty cold in winter, which explained the presence of a large eiderdown stowed on a shelf at the back of the shed. There were one or two bits of ill-matched cutlery, two plates and an assortment of mugs in a shallow tray next to the washing-up bowl. A box of candles, some teabags, a jam jar full of sugar and a kettle constituted the rest of the basic domestic equipment. Prominently displayed on a hook by the window was a large green first aid box with a white cross on it. The only item that had no obvious practical use was a rather grainy black-and-white picture of an attractive young woman hanging on the wall. Steve took this to be Judy, so he determined not to bring it up in conversation.

While Steve was taking it all in, Stan had put some water in the kettle and put it on the gas ring. He then methodically selected two mugs and put a tea bag in each before announcing.

"I've got milk. I haven't got any biscuits, Gran wouldn't let me bring some today, but I got milk from the fridge," Stan said, taking a small plastic bottle from a rucksack hung on the wall.

Steve watched as his host carefully made up two mugs of tea and then offered one to him. Turning down the offer of sugar, Steve put a dash of milk in his tea. He was a little surprised to see that Stan didn't take sugar either, so he obviously kept that for guests.

"I like Georgia. Are you going to marry her?"

Steve was surprised by the abruptness of the question, but he found the older man's reluctance to beat about the bush quite refreshing.

"I guess we might one day. We are both very much in love, so we might get married, but we haven't made any firm plans. We'll just see how things go."

Steve was quite surprised at his own frankness; here he was, talking openly about his love for Georgia, but he got the impression that Stan was not one for small talk.

"I love my girlfriend Judy, but she's gone away with the army. I hope she comes back soon; I don't want to live with Gran forever. I get on her nerves sometimes. I try hard, but I get things wrong a lot, and it upsets her, and I have to leave her on her own for a while until she's better. She works hard to look after me. But I get under her feet, and I can be a nuisance."

The picture that Stan was painting of his domestic arrangements was strangely at odds with what Georgia had said, and Steve felt extremely sad to think of the older man putting up with a loveless relationship with his gran while he waited with a picture of a girlfriend who would never be coming back. The two men sat in silence for a while before Stan, having finished his tea, stood up and took a small plastic bag from his rucksack.

"My friends will be here for dinner soon," he announced before walking over to one of the benches in the graveyard.

Steve dutifully followed, and they sat together on the bench where the older man untied the top of the plastic bag that appeared to hold a lot of small pieces of bread and bits of cut-up bacon rind.

"They won't be long. They might be shy with you here, but it's their time."

Steve suddenly noticed a small group of large black birds wheeling in the sky above the church. Stan knocked on the arm of the bench repeatedly with his knuckle and threw the contents of the bag onto the path, some six feet from the bench. A jackdaw, which appeared less cautious than the rest, flew down first and started to pick out some of the more desirable scraps.

"That's Paddy," explained Stan. "He's one of my best friends. He sometimes joins me in the shed if I leave the door open. He likes to sit on the arm of the bench here for special treats, but I don't think he will if you're here."

By this time, the rest of the birds had descended in order to squabble over the scraps before they were all gone. Stan sat, completely content, smiling at the small gathering on the floor. When the last of them had cleared the remnants of food and flown off, he carefully folded the plastic bag and put it in his pocket. He smiled at Steve, produced a small piece of what looked like chicken from a piece of folded tissue he'd taken from another pocket and placed it on the arm of the bench beside him. The couple sat in silence for a while, and then a bird that Steve took to be Paddy flew down and landed on the arm of the bench next to Stan to investigate what was obviously a tempting morsel. The bird stood for a while, and Steve could clearly see its grey hood with a silvery sheen to the back of its head. Its piercing silvery-white eyes stood out as it cocked its head from side to side to investigate the chicken and Steve before jabbing forward and picking it up. To Steve's surprise, it did not rush to fly off but stood for some seconds with its beak full of the chunk of chicken. It continued to look at the two men on the bench and then suddenly flew off to a local tree, presumably to eat his reward in peace, leaving Steve with a real sense of privilege at having shared the experience.

"Paddy likes you. He won't forget you now."

"I think he's pretty great too. Do you have other friends here?"

"Oh yes. Lots. I've got lots of friends. I'm very lucky."

"Who are your other friends?" pressed Steve.

"I see lots of them. The squirrels you met yesterday. Hedgehogs, mice, lots of little birds and Judy, of course."

"Judy?"

"Yes. Judy is my robin friend. I named her after my friend Judy."

"And any other friends?" prompted Steve in an attempt to steer the conversation away from the missing girlfriend.

"The fox family are often around; they like to play among the gravestones or just to sunbathe on the lawn. Sometimes when I'm here late, they will come very close. If I've got something special for them, like a bit of meat, the mother fox, she's called a vixen, will come up to me and take it for her young ones. On those evenings, I sometimes see Sahi. She used to come here a lot, but I don't see her much now. She never came for food; she just flew past looking for her own dinner. She likes to fly up and down the river looking for mice on the bank. She's very quiet, and sometimes she surprises me when she flies past. Some people are frightened of owls, but they are nice birds."

"Sahi?"

"Sahi is the barn owl. I hear other owls a lot, but I don't see them very often. They don't come for dinner. I've got a new friend, Harry. He flies down low over the reeds, but I don't feed him. He gets his own dinner, like the owls.

"Harry?"

"Yes, Harry the harrier," he explained, with a rare smile at his own inventiveness. I think he lives over in the nature park, but sometimes he flies along the river bank. Sometimes, if I've upset Gran, I come down late and stay until it's dark, and that's when I see the hedgehogs. It's nice here at night, and sometimes I fall asleep, and I have to sneak back into the house when it's late. If it's really late, I go into the shed and have a sleep in my chair so I don't wake Gran and upset her. It's different here at night, lots of friends and nobody to disturb them. They don't mind me staying here at night, and I sometimes fall asleep on the bench here and wake up to find the hedgehogs snuffling around underneath.

"And do you see a lot of bats?" queried Steve before adding, "We often see them down by the lychgate in the evening."

"I see them, but they're not my friends. They just flitter about a bit and don't stay around. Friends don't just keep disappearing like that; they stop for a meal or a cup of tea."

"With so many mouths to feed, it must cost you a fortune every week."

"I manage to sneak things out of the house. Sometimes, I don't eat all my dinner and put bits in one of my little plastic bags. I don't tell Gran because she would be upset at me wasting food. I don't like to be a nuisance for Gran, so I try to take some food without her knowing. Karen at the shop is very kind. She's my friend. Sometimes, she saves some of the things they have to throw out. They're not rotten, but they can't sell them. I sometimes get a loaf of bread or even sausage rolls; Paddy loves a bit of sausage roll," he said with a smile. "And when I got some cheese slices, everyone seemed to like them. I sometimes move barrels about for Tony at the pub and do other jobs, and he will give me a pint when I go in the pub. If he has anything customers have left on their plates, he will let me have that for my friends as well."

As the pair sat and enjoyed the tranquillity of the graveyard, Steve couldn't help but marvel at the way Stan put so much of his energy into looking after the place and all its inhabitants. Paddy's visit and that of the squirrels the previous day had shown how Stan's gentle caring nature had won over the trust of so many of his friends. His thoughts were disrupted by Stan's abrupt declaration that he had to get on with his work, and he diligently set off to collect tools from the shed. Steve sat for a while before deciding that he would go back to the flower shop to see if he could grab some lunch.

Georgia and her mum were busy putting together some flower orders for their regular customers when Steve arrived back at the shop. Rita had apparently taken the van to pick up some items from a wholesaler in town. Steve looked at the prepared arrangements standing in buckets of water by the door.

"I don't know how you manage to put together such lovely displays so quickly," he commented. "Whenever I try it, the whole thing looks like a dog's breakfast."

"A few basic rules and lots of experience," explained Georgia. "Do you want me to give you some lessons?"

"No thanks, I'll stick to things I'm good at and start lunch."

He made his way up to the flat and put the kettle on before preparing some sandwiches. Georgia had given him instructions that morning on where the ingredients were for the meal. Steven was aware that they always had a simple lunch, so they could quickly interrupt it if any customers called. The shop didn't rely much on passing trade, but they wanted to be available in case anyone suddenly had the urge to buy some flowers or a potted plant. When he had prepared the meal, he called down for the workers to come up for their lunch. Both Georgia and her mum were ready for a break and were pleased to sit down to the meal that had been set up. As they ate, Steve outlined how he had spent the morning wandering around the village and in particular he recalled his meeting with Stan.

"That guy has no idea how badly his grandmother is treating him," he commented. "He seems to think she's doing him some big favour; she doesn't appear to do anything to make his life comfortable. She treats him as if he's in a cheap bed and breakfast place or even a hostel, chucking him out for most of the day. That shed of his is more of a home to him than the room he has with his gran. It's pathetic to hear him saying how he has to sneak food out of the house for the animals in the graveyard, and it's obvious that she never gives him enough money."

"There's never been any love lost there on her part," said Clara. "And it's awful to think that he has money of his own. Apart from his disability allowance, he got some compensation after the accident, so he shouldn't be going short. He's not exactly loaded, but he should have a comfortable lifestyle, but that nasty woman won't let him have access to it. She claims that she is looking after his money so that he doesn't waste it all. All the village know the true situation, but apparently there is nothing we can do about it as Stan doesn't complain; he even defends the obnoxious old hag. No, Martha Turner is quite a hate figure because Stan is liked by the villagers, and we can't stand to see him being mistreated in such a way. She doesn't go short; every week she has us deliver a large arrangement of flowers and never the cheaper varieties. I don't like going round to deliver them, but business is business. Each time I go, she comes to the door and holds me in some trivial conversation, making time for any observer to see the quality of her flowers. She then goes in and puts them on the front room windowsill so anyone passing will see them. I've told her it's not the best place for them, but she wants them on show."

The trio sat and finished their sandwiches, and Georgia poured each of them another cup of tea. Steve looked down at the few remaining scraps of the sandwich on his plate, and he had an idea.

"I could take the remnants of our meal, the bits of crust and the fat I cut off the cooked ham, and take them over to Stan for his friends."

"Better still," added Clara, "why don't you pop into the shop and see if Hannah Cordwell can sell you any bread that is coming to the end of its shelf-life? If not, you could always buy a small loaf for the birds and perhaps some biscuits for Stan. I'd like to contribute to our local wildlife hero. And while we are talking about the wildlife, as it's the last day of your holiday, why don't the pair of you have a wild-ish evening at the pub, and I'll give Georgia a special bonus to support your revelry?"

"Thanks, Daisy," he said, giving her a kiss on the cheek. "That's very kind of you, and if Georgia and I ever do get married, we will make sure all the flowers are provided by you."

"That's very kind of you, love, and I would ensure that you got family discount for the big day."

Having accepted the money that Clara had forced upon him and giving Georgia a more substantial kiss, he set off to face the challenge of Hannah Cordwell.

When he arrived at the general store, he noticed that Karen was busy rearranging some items on the shelves while an older woman was at the till. He took this to be the famous Mrs Cordwell, and he was right.

"Hello, you must be Georgia's friend," she gushed. "So, how can I help you?"

"Yes, I'm Georgia's partner," he corrected her. "And as I was coming in to buy some biscuits, I was just wondering if you have any bread suitable for feeding the birds?"

"Karen is just labelling some reduced items now if you want to have a look through them. We like to do our bit to support the local wildlife," she added, with an unctuous smile.

He went over and selected two packets of plain biscuits and a small carton of long-life milk and then stood, or rather hovered, over the young assistant. It reminded him of the shopping expeditions he had made with Georgia as a student. They knew when each of the local supermarkets had their 'sell by' days, and they would wait like vultures to see what little gems were reduced. It meant that for much of the time, they had never had a fixed schedule of what they would eat in a week but would decide upon the menu when they saw what was available on the day, like a pair of modern-day hunter-gatherers. It wasn't the best of hunting today, but he was able to get a packet of hot cross buns and a rather battered small, sliced loaf and took his purchases over to Mrs Cordwell.

"Now, what have you got there, love?" she asked with that same smile that appeared uncomfortably over-friendly to Stan. "Let me see. You can have the buns at the marked reduced price, but the loaf really looks too knocked about to sell, so you can have that for free for the birds."

Well pleased with his acquisitions and not wishing to linger in the shop, he thanked the shopkeeper, accepted the instruction to 'have a nice day' and set off towards the church. He couldn't resist calling in briefly at the flower shop to show Georgia and her mum what he had bought.

"Hot cross buns and a small loaf for the birds, and biscuits and milk for Stan," he declared before adding,

"That Mrs Cordwell is a very friendly lady. I can understand why her husband might have been a bit concerned about her over-affectionate nature."

"I can see that I'm going to have to limit your shopping expeditions," commented Georgia. "But on the plus side, you might get a discount on our shopping bill."

"Once you get into the swing of it, perhaps you could do some of my weekly shopping as well," added Clara.

"Thanks for your faith in my purchasing power, Daisy," he said with a smile. "But it's not an enterprise that I wish to consider. Now, if you'll excuse me, I have some items to deliver to Stan."

He left the shop and walked across the road to the lychgate. He stood for a moment in the carved oak structure and looked at some of the details on it. He couldn't estimate its age with any accuracy, but he reckoned that it must be a couple of hundred years old at least. He couldn't help but wonder when it last served its original purpose of being a covered place to rest the coffin or for mourners to shelter before the burial service. That was in the days when most people died at home and were carried or transported on a bier, nowadays people were usually taken to their funeral in a hearse, and many lychgates had simply become places offering shelter from the elements for young people to meet in the evening.

Steve walked on into the graveyard. He was never a religious person, but there was something peaceful about such places which made rushing around seem out of place, even disrespectful, so he strolled along the path casually reading some of the inscriptions on the graves. Many of the more ornate memorials were still relatively easy to read after a couple of centuries, while some of the less ostentatious stones bore indecipherable marks, offering no information about the identity of the deceased. The families of the occupants of such plots had probably spent all they could on a cheap stone, and it's likely that the friends and relatives of the deceased had themselves died before the gravestone became a blank record of yet another unknown villager.

There was no sign of Stan in the churchyard, so Steve went directly to the shed, where he found his friend sitting in the armchair and sharpening a pair of shears.

"Hi Stan, I just got a couple of items from the shop for your friends and some milk and biscuits for your store cupboard."

"That's kind," he said as he examined his gifts. "Paddy will love some pieces from the buns. I'll put some out when he comes tomorrow. Would you like a cup of tea?"

He didn't wait for an answer and, after taking off his gloves, set about filling the kettle. He followed the same methodical routine and soon presented Steve with a cup of tea. Once again, Steve was relieved to note that it was indeed a very nice cup of tea.

"Would you like a biscuit?" said Stan, offering the opened packet.

"No thanks, Stan. I've just recently had lunch."

"Paddy will be pleased about the buns. He'll be back tomorrow. He knows when his food will be ready. Sometimes, I haven't got anything for him if Gran won't let me take anything from the house, but Paddy still comes to see me and will stay for a while. When it's time for their feeds, some of the big birds call out to remind me. They know I'm a friend. It's sad when I haven't got anything for my friends, but they know I still want to help them. They're good friends."

The pair sat for a while chatting, largely about Stan's friends and the feeding routine they appeared to have adopted, but eventually Steve had to make his apologies and set off back to the florists. As he left, he couldn't help but notice that Stan had consumed over half the packet of biscuits, and it was obvious that he had been pretty hungry.

The bar at the Trout Inn was relatively quiet when Georgia and Steve arrived that evening, where they were greeted by the landlord, Tony.

"Good evening, you're the lucky young man that's looking after our Georgia," he said. "And what can I get you?"

"Two large glasses of Shiraz, please," replied Steve.

"I've known Tony for years," explained Georgia. "I had my first drink in here when I was old enough to come in."

"And a few times before you were old enough, as I recall," added the landlord with a wink.

"Perhaps, but you weren't too concerned about such details; as long as we were well-behaved, we could get the odd half of shandy. I guess it's a bit different with our local police officer trying to flex his law-enforcing muscles. Daft Danny Bright would nick his own grandmother to make himself look big."

"Yes, he's a pain," agreed Tony. "He has a habit of coming in here, sometimes in uniform, and he stares around as if he's on some kind of mission. He likes to think that he's the big detective figure, but he couldn't detect an in-grown toenail if you told him which foot it was on. He's so busy trying to put on a show that he just makes himself look ridiculous."

"He's just a pathetic figure," agreed Georgia. "But then, he was like that, even at school; he was always intent upon joining the police. While he was in junior school, he got hold of his grandmother's outdated bus pass and printed *Plees* on it in blue felt-tip pen. He used the same pen to draw a police helmet on her picture and then flashed his 'warrant card' in a vain attempt to impress people. It wouldn't surprise me if he still carried the same identification today because I still find it hard to accept that the real police would have issued him with any official way of showing that he might have any authority within the force. He was always one of those annoying individuals who thought he was much cleverer than he actually was. He would go crawling to the teacher to grass up anybody who was doing anything even slightly naughty. I know that Mrs Cooper in the upper juniors got sick to death of him reporting every child's misdemeanours, and in the end, she would just tell him to go and sit down, even before he'd had time to disclose what one of his classmates might have done."

It was at this point that Steve caught sight of the subject of their conversation entering the pub. He was not in uniform, but Steve recognised the young man he had seen patrolling the mean streets of Hartbridge that morning.

"So, you've been coming in here for some time then, darling?" he interjected in an attempt to close down the conversation about police incompetence in the village.

"Yes, I have," she replied, having observed Steve's discreet nod in the direction of the new customer. "I remember coming in during the summer months as a young girl with Mum and Dad. We used to have lunch outside sometimes, and Dad would walk down to the river with me and warn me of the possible dangers of swimming in it. Apparently, he'd had a friend who had been tempted to go for a swim on one particularly hot afternoon and drowned. The river often looks very inviting in hot weather, but it can be dangerous to venture in. Those warm sunny days I spent down here are some of the few recollections I have of Dad."

Without bothering to engage Danny Bright in conversation, the couple took their drinks out to the garden and sat at one of the picnic tables that were set out on the lawn. It was obvious why the bar had been sparsely populated because most of the clientele had decided to enjoy the warm summer evening and the beautiful views down to the river and beyond.

"You never seem to talk about your father much," he observed, careful not to make it seem like a direct question, seeking an answer.

"No. The truth is that I don't remember much about him. I must have been about five when he and Mum split up. I don't remember clearly what happened over that, but even as a young child, I was aware of a lot of tension. The older villagers don't talk about it to me, but I have heard the odd snippets of conversation, and I suspect that Dad had been having an affair with someone. Then again, I've told you how people round here like a bit of a scandal to gossip about, and even if there isn't anything going on, there are plenty who would make something up. You know what childhood memories are like; you remember certain events. I remember coming to the pub for meals in the garden, and I remember other things like my pink teddy bear and falling in the garden, cutting my head open. I clearly recall my first day at primary school, feeling so small in a mass of bigger pupils. My early life seems to be recalled as if in jumbled-up short extracts from a video, and all the bits in between have been erased. People in the village never mention my father to me, perhaps because they feel the subject of the divorce will upset me.

"The fact is, I've been very happy being brought up by Mum, and I've never been curious about Dad. Perhaps that's why I've never asked her about him. From what limited conversations I've had with Mum, it's clear that Dad never wanted children, and my arrival was hardly the highlight of his life. Mind you, Mum makes no secret of the fact that she never had any strong maternal instincts and openly admits that I was not entirely planned for. She still concedes that she was never driven to be a mother, but she's made up for that by being my best friend. There have been the odd times when I have wondered what it would be like to have a father, but I've never felt deprived. We were lucky that Dad never shirked his financial responsibility for my upbringing, and he kept up his payments right up to the time I was twenty. He was never quite so diligent with recognising my birthdays, but I always got money at Christmas. I guess it wasn't a 'normal' family setup, but it worked for us."

"It's funny how we are led to believe what constitutes a normal family unit," observed Steve. "I suppose that my family would seem pretty standard, with my having a mum and dad, but they weren't your average couple, and for years I got very mixed messages from them as to how I should lead my life. Mum had a very strong belief in her religious faith and was very clear about what constituted bad behaviour. She would regale me with images of what would happen to me if I was naughty. When I was apprehended after I had helped myself to a biscuit from the pantry, I was made to feel as if the Devil himself had already started stoking up a furnace just for me. Dad was much more laid back; he was still a very moral person and brought me up to respect others, but he appreciated that we can all show signs of weakness at times. So, for much of the time, Mum was a lone figure in our little family; I'm sure that she loved us both, but she had great difficulty overlooking what she saw as our frailties."

The conversation was brought to a close as Mark rushed over to their table. His face, as ever, was a picture of cheerfulness, and he was keen to talk to Georgia.

"Hello, beautiful lady. I have a joke for you; it's a smashing joke."

"Go on then, what is it?" asked Georgia as she prepared to face up to yet another of Mark's 'smashing' jokes.

"What kind of shoes do frogs wear?" and before anyone could answer, he called out, "Open toad." Then, laughing heartily, he moved on to 'entertain' the people at another table.

"That's not bad for Mark," observed Georgia. "At least he got the punchline right. He sometimes mixes his jokes up a bit, and it becomes very confusing, but he still laughs like a drain, and it's infectious. His dad always keeps an eye on him, and if he starts to get on people's nerves, then Colin calms him down."

As if he had heard his name, Mark ran over with a continuation of his floor show.

"Hello again, beautiful lady. What do you call a person with no body and no nose?" In the silence that followed, he shrugged his shoulders and said, "Nobody knows."

While it would be true to say that neither element in his act had brought the house down, Mark was delighted, and he closed his turn in the time-honoured way.

"Thank you, ladies and gentlemen, you've been a wonderful audience," and then he wandered back to rejoin his dad.

The young couple didn't stay late at the pub because Steve was aware of his need to get an early start the next day. As they strolled the short distance back to the flat, they shared a general air of contentment. It had been a pleasant day, and Steve was looking forward to earning some money in his temporary job. He couldn't help the feeling of being on the threshold of a new phase in their lives together. He found the prospect very pleasing, and he stopped and impulsively kissed her gently.

CHAPTER THREE

Steve had some difficulty getting up the following morning. He never liked getting up early and leaving Georgia in bed was never something he relished. As he sat on the side of the bed, his thoughts were of the times in his student digs when, after a romantic evening together, they'd had to get up so he could walk her home. He had hated having to break into the beauty of an idyllic time with her and longed for the day when they could spend the entire night together. Instead, the price of sharing a few hours together was to face the two-mile walk back to her lodgings after midnight, where he would have to suffer another parting before making the return trip to his own place. He became a regular figure, trudging back to his digs in the early hours of the morning. He was once stopped by a police patrol car to enquire after his reason for being out so late. The officers obviously identified with his situation and left him to get on with his journey. After that, the officers regularly acknowledged him on his late-night trek, and he often hoped that they might offer to give him a lift if they were going his way, but it was clear that the local constabulary did not offer a taxi service. The lengthy walks back to his digs had not been much fun, particularly on the cold, wet winter nights, but the worst part of the experience was that Georgia had not been able to stay overnight. That was behind them now, and he felt good.

Despite her protestations that she would get up and have a bit of breakfast with him, he convinced her to stay where she was, and he quickly made himself a piece of toast and a coffee before returning to the bedroom.

"What about the idea that I should call in sick?" he asked in a less than serious attempt to prolong his morning with her. "The plant wouldn't grind to a halt if I didn't turn up."

"While I have to agree with your argument and the underlying sentiment, I would suggest that failure to turn up on your first day could be viewed in a dim light by your employers," she replied. "And we need the money."

Reluctantly accepting the inevitable, he kissed her before dramatically adding, "Work is the curse of the loving classes," and setting off for his day's toil.

It was a glorious summer's day, and even as he waited for his early bus, Steve was sure it was going to be hot. He hadn't been waiting long before Mark turned up and beamed when he saw his new friend.

"Morning, Mark, waiting for the bus?" Steve greeted him.

"Yes, day centre minibus picks me up. Won't be long. Celia, my fiancée, will be at the centre. My Celia is beautiful."

The two friends sat for a while on the bench in the warming sunshine before Steve decided to promote a conversation by introducing one of Mark's special areas of interest.

"I've got a couple of jokes for you, Mark. What's brown and sticky?"

He waited a few seconds while Mark looked bemused before giving the answer, "A stick."

Mark looked a bit confused for a minute and then laughed loudly before repeating the punchline as if to imprint it on his memory and enjoy the joke all over again. Steve took the opportunity to build on the 'hilarity' of his first riddle with a quick follow-up.

"And here's another one for you. What do you call a boomerang that won't come back?" This time, he didn't wait long before giving the answer, "A stick." He wasn't sure how much Mark had understood the joke but after a short while, he laughed gleefully and was still laughing when his minibus arrived and he climbed aboard, probably with the intent of treating his friends to his 'smashing' new jokes. Steve's bus arrived shortly afterwards, and he set off towards his first day to help bring in the harvest.

His first experience of 'agricultural' work was not one of toiling under the hot sun wearing a smock and chewing a piece of straw before stopping for a flagon of cider, a wedge of cheese and a hunk of crusty bread. Instead, he found himself in a very large, noisy factory with the constant pressure to keep up with the pace of the machinery to ensure the freshness of the goods that were eventually spewed out as tens of thousands of packets of frozen peas. He was more than ready for his lunch break when he was able to go out into the fresh air with a number of co-workers to consume their respective sandwiches and generally lark about. As Steve sat on a pile of pallets in the yard, he was approached by another young man who politely asked if he might be able to share the improvised seating. The two young workers sat for a while, eating their respective lunches, and the newcomer introduced himself.

"Hi, I'm Don. I'm here during the university break to try to reduce my need to run up even higher student debts. I've just finished my second year, and I'm shocked at the amount I will have to pay back on my student loan. You're obviously new; are you doing holiday work as well?"

"Not exactly. I finished university recently, but my partner and I haven't managed to secure any long-term employment, so this is a way of getting by for a few weeks while we continue looking for something more suitable. My name's Steve, by the way."

"I should have been finished at uni by now, but I took a year out after I left school. I had thought I would try and get a bit of work to put money aside before I went away, but then

I got the offer of a 'cheap' back-packing wander around Australia with the opportunities to work my way around in a variety of manual jobs. It seems that the jobs were not as numerous as I had been led to believe, but the partying was pretty good, so I started my later studies with no money at all."

"We didn't have a year out, and we still have virtually nothing and obscene debts," commented Steve. "But fortunately my partner's mum has a shop in Hartbridge, and we have a flat there. It's been a godsend while we look round for permanent work so we can have our own place at some time in the distant future."

"So, how are you finding your introduction to the world of work?"

"It's very different to university life. Obviously, it's hard physically, and the constant pressure of being driven by the pace of the conveyors makes this lunch break much appreciated. I've no doubt that I will get used to it, but what I have found hard so far is the need to be up at some ridiculous time in the morning to catch the early bus. By the time I get back in the village, I will have been away for nearly eleven hours. On top of that, I have the torment of having to leave my girlfriend in the morning as she prepares to enjoy an extra hour in bed."

"I pass through Hartbridge on my way to and from work; why don't I give you a lift? I could pick you up at eight, and you would be back in the village by half past five. That is, assuming that my car keeps chugging along. My aunt gave it to me when she gave up driving, so I can't complain, but every journey is an adventure."

"Sounds ideal to me, Don. That will make my life a lot easier, and I can contribute to the petrol money."

"If you insist. I'll see you at the end of the shift in the car park."

Thus it was that the two young men headed home that evening in Don's old car and exchanged views on the nature of the work at the food processing plant.

"The work is completely different to university life," observed Don, "and is physically demanding until you get used to it, but it pays well, and it's only for the summer season. The other advantage for me in coming home is that I can play for the village cricket team. I don't claim to be particularly good. I class myself as an all-rounder; I'm a very average batsman, my bowling is pathetic, and my fielding is patchy, but I love the game, and they are always short of players. I don't suppose you play, do you?"

"I played at school and in my first year at university, but after that I found other things to do in the summer," answered Steve, who was being somewhat modest in that he had, in fact, been a more than competent player. They had tried to persuade him to stick with the team at university, but he found the prospect of spending his time with Georgia was infinitely preferable to hanging around with a group of men on the weekend. Georgia had offered to help with the teas at matches so she could share his hobby in some small way, but he'd recognised that this constituted a considerable sacrifice for her, so the cricket had to go.

"Do you fancy the odd game with the village team at some time?"

"I might, but am I eligible? I've only just arrived, and I don't know how long we will be staying."

"There's no problem with eligibility; we call ourselves a village team, but more than half the team don't live in the village."

"OK, I'll have a word with my partner before I commit myself."

"She's more than welcome to come along and watch if she's free. Let me know tomorrow if you are available, and I'll have a word with Bill Norton, the captain of the team. I'm sure he would be delighted to have a bit of fresh blood in the squad. Bill absolutely lives for his cricket and takes it all very seriously, but the rest of the guys still have fun."

Don delivered Steve to the door of the flower shop, and it was a bit of a surprise for Georgia and Rita, who were not expecting him back so soon. After Rita had gone home, the young couple sat down with a cup of tea and shared information about their experiences during the day. While Georgia had enjoyed a relatively easy day working alongside Rita and chatting about village life, Steve recounted how exhausted he was after a day of hard manual work and watching rivers of peas floating before him.

"Who was that who dropped you off this evening," she asked.

"That was Don; he's kindly arranged to provide a lift for me to and from work. It saves quite a lot of time. I enjoy the bus journey, but it does take in just about every village in the county before getting to the factory. The biggest bonus is that I will get to have nearly an hour longer with you in the morning."

"I thought I recognised the driver, Don Aspen; his parents live up the other end of the village. His mother worked as a GP in Callerthorpe, and his father was a lawyer or something."

"Is there anything you don't know about this village and its inhabitants?"

"I spent most of my school career in the same classes as Don; in fact, we eventually went out together for a while. He chose to have a gap year before going off to university."

"So, now all your sordid little secrets are coming out," he teased her.

"If by sordid, you mean a quick kiss after youth club, then I'm guilty as charged. The truth is, we were only together for a short time. It almost seemed inevitable as we had spent so much time together, but it was never a serious romance, and the split-up was nothing dramatic. We just sort of drifted back into just being friends. We didn't even go to the school prom together."

"So, you went to the prom with yet another of your many boyfriends? And to think that I never had any girlfriends before you," he said with feigned innocence.

"Of course, I believe you, just as I believed you when you insisted that the Pope played centre forward for Arsenal for a while."

"It wasn't his best season, and playing in his full papal robes, while it might have encouraged good fortune from a higher authority, didn't help his scoring rate. I think that's why many Arsenal fans were not disappointed when he moved to Lazio and prefer to forget the whole incident. While we are on the subject of sport, your very good friend Don asked if I might be interested in playing for the local cricket team, but I said I would have to discuss it with you first."

"I have no objections to that," she said before giggling and continuing, "It would be nice to go along and watch Don play. As it happens, I found your cricket trousers recently and nearly threw them out; they're so covered in grass stains, but I might be able to get some stain-remover on them and get you to at least look like a cricketer."

After a heavy week's work, during which he became sick to death of the sight of peas, Steve was grateful for the opportunity to get a bit of fresh air and to play for the village team. Decked out in his cricket trousers and a white shirt, he strolled down to the ground with Georgia and, after finding her a seat with one or two of her friends, he walked over to the pavilion to be introduced to the rest of the team. The captain had been more than willing to get an extra young player for the team, and Don had arranged for them to meet up at the cricket pavilion at one o'clock. Steve was introduced to the other members of the team, who seemed a pretty disparate group. They appeared to range between sixteen and sixty. Some looked relatively fit, while others looked in better shape to watch cricket than to play it. The captain, Bill Norton, was the head teacher of a local school, in his fifties, and he was delighted to meet up with his new team member and to include him in the group discussion before the game. In the pep talk, the captain insisted upon addressing his team members as 'gentlemen', and he reminded them that this was an important match against a Callerthorpe team that included a number of young men from the army college there. Steve was informed that he would bat at number ten as the captain hadn't had a chance to see if his new recruit was any good.

Callerthorpe won the toss and elected to bat first, scoring a very respectable two hundred and nine all out. Bill Norton had naturally opened the bowling and had shown himself to be a respectable medium-paced player. Throughout his numerous bowling spells, he had signalled for his team members to go to various specific positions as he set the field. He did this in an authoritative manner, like some vastly experienced international captain. Steve had taken two catches, each of which elicited enthusiastic clapping from Georgia. The truth is that he would have had difficulty missing either of the catches which had been gently hit straight towards him. Naturally, Captain Bill opened the batting for Hartbridge, and he scored steadily while others were systematically dismissed around him. The score had reached two hundred and four when Steve was sent out to bat. Bill Norton sauntered down to meet his new young partner and, in a hushed tone, gave his instructions.

"We only need six to win, so all you need to do is block the remaining four balls, and then it will give me the chance to face up for the next over. Just remember, no heroics, take it steady."

Steve took his guard and faced up to the bowler. The village pitch was not the smooth, regular sort of surface he was used to, but he had seen this bowler in action, and he didn't pose much of a threat. Steve had every intention of following the captain's game plan, and he prepared to block the first delivery. The ball came down slowly and was begging to be knocked over the boundary. Steve braced himself to give the ball the treatment it warranted, but before it reached him, it bounced off a particular irregularity on the pitch, and his majestic sweep barely connected with it. He had no idea where it had gone, and for a moment, he stood transfixed, trying to work out what had happened to the ball. He was relieved to see it skidding off to the boundary.

The umpire duly signified four runs, which caused Georgia to applaud enthusiastically. Steve looked up at his captain, who was less than impressed by the wild stroke his new young player had attempted. Bill Norton was standing at the other end of the wicket, slowly shaking his head from side to side. Steve wasn't going to risk anything too dramatic on that pitch, and when the next ball came down, he played the solid blocking stroke that his captain had asked for. The gentle defensive shot only caused the ball to move forward a few yards, so he was surprised to hear the captain shouting for a run. For a moment he was in two minds. He took a couple of strides down the pitch before changing his mind and starting to resume his position by the wickets, but then he saw Bill charging towards him, so he set off as one of the fielders ran in to collect the ball and throw it towards the stumps ahead of the young batsman. Desperately, Steve threw himself full length towards the crease, which proved unnecessary as the misdirected ball flew harmlessly past the stumps and careered off to the boundary for four overthrows. The game was won, and the winning runs were credited to Steve.

The captain was not entirely pleased at the manner of the victory, but in the bar of the Trout Inn after the game there was a general acceptance of the fact that the new player hadn't performed too badly. Bill Norton drew Steve aside at one point and apologised for calling for the last single, admitting that it was the fact that he hadn't trusted the younger player. Steve realised that Bill took his cricket very seriously, and he would often steer any conversation around to the game he obviously venerated. All of the team enjoyed playing, but Bill almost lived for cricket, and he personally spent hours during the summer months tending his precious pitch. He even arranged for a small group of the senior boys in his school to opt for his own 'Sports Ground Management Course' as an alternative to games lessons in the summer months. The initials SGMC looked good on the master timetable in his office, but all it entailed was the boys catching a bus to Hartbridge with a member of the support staff where they would tend to his beloved pitch. This involved cutting the grass with an antique push mower and walking up and down the strip with a heavy roller, which Bill had mysteriously acquired when another school in the county had sold off some of their grounds and no longer had a cricket pitch. It was in a similar fashion that Bill had come by the two sight screens, which, like the pavilion, were regularly painted by those on the Sports Ground Management Course.

After a couple of drinks, most of the cricketers had left, so Steve suggested that he and Georgia might take their drinks outside, and they were ready for a quiet evening when Mark arrived with his dad. With his usual beaming smile, Mark ran over to Georgia.

"Hello, sweet, beautiful lady. I've got a smashing joke," he announced before going straight into his routine. "What's brown and sticky?"

As Georgia honestly didn't know what the answer was, she shrugged her shoulders, only to be informed.

"A boomerang." Mark chuckled to himself at his own ability to tell good jokes and walked back to see his father.

"It's a long story, darling. I'll explain it later," said Steve in response to her quizzical gaze.

For the rest of the evening, the guests in the pub garden were periodically treated to Mark's floor show as he recounted his apparently endless repertoire of jokes, some of which made sense and none of which were particularly funny, but his enthusiastic delivery had the customers laughing. Eventually, Colin signified that the show had to finish, so he informed his son that it was bedtime, and the pair made their departure with Mark dramatically blowing kisses to his audience as he was escorted from the 'stage'.

Steve and Georgia didn't stay late at the pub because he had to be up early the next day for work. It had been a very enjoyable evening, and as the couple set off towards the flower shop, they discussed how lucky they were to be able to live in such a pleasant environment; the road was devoid of traffic, and there was a reassuring silence. It was so unlike the busy streets around Steve's parents' home, where it would be tantamount to suicide to walk along the middle of the road on the way home from the pub and where the sound of traffic along the nearby motorway went on twenty-four hours a day. It was a time that they were intent upon enjoying because they both knew that one day they would have to become grown-ups and move into 'proper' jobs as soon as some enlightened employer recognised their talents. This would undoubtedly necessitate a move away from Hartbridge because his degree in marine biology and hers in the performing arts had no obvious value in a small inland village.

Over the next few weeks, the couple got into a regular routine of Steve working at the factory and Georgia in the shop. While he worked overtime on the occasional Saturday to get extra money, they tried to keep their Sundays free and generally went out to the Trout on Sunday evenings to meet up with friends. One Monday, the pattern of village life changed; Steve returned home to be met by Georgia with some disturbing news.

"Martha Turner is dead," she announced as soon as he came into the shop. "Rita saw a lot of emergency vehicles outside the house on her way in to work this morning, so she felt obliged to find out if Stan and his gran were OK. Daft Danny was on scene guard, and of course he was delighted to show how informed he was about the incident. He was standing there behind his blue and white police tape, trying to look important while the real police were inside. Apparently, because it was an unexplained death and there'd been some sort of head injury, they'd brought in some real detectives from town. Rita couldn't get any more information, but it seems that Stan is fine, but a bit shocked because he had been the one to find his gran when he came downstairs to the kitchen this morning."

"Poor old Stan, it must have been a hell of a shock. Obviously, she was a right tartar, but he didn't see it that way. He'll miss her," observed Steve.

"A number of people have been into the shop with updates, but not much is known. The local grapevine isn't what it used to be. The police have asked for a pathologist's report to establish the time of death, but the preliminary inspection suggested sometime late yesterday morning and no later than two."

"So she'd been lying there for nearly a full day?"

"It would appear so, but then you know how Stan didn't like to disturb his gran. Most of the time when he was indoors, he would be in his room. He possibly got home last night and went straight upstairs so as not to annoy Martha, not knowing that she was lying dead in the kitchen. He probably just went to the kitchen to get some bits of food for his friends before he left for work this morning. The detectives, in their dubious wisdom, set Danny out to collect information from anyone who might have noticed anything out of the ordinary. Danny has been out, proudly informing residents that he was on 'house-to-house enquires' as though it's some sort of secret police code terminology. The truth is that he gives out as much information as he takes in, and he likes to infer that he has already established what has happened. It's sort of reassuring to know that we have such a fine member of the constabulary among us. I guess we'll have to get down to the pub this evening to see what's been going on. PC Bright will no doubt be there to bathe in his moment of glory as part of the 'massive' police operation, if not to try and give the impression that he's running it."

The pub was quite full that evening as many of the villagers gathered to find out what had happened to Mrs Turner. Quite by chance, and certainly not by design, Georgia and Steve found themselves at the bar next to Danny Bright, who was talking to the landlord. It was clear that the young police officer had consumed a few pints, and he was even less discreet than usual as he outlined his conclusion as to what had happened the previous day.

"It was probably your standard domestic," he was explaining. "Stan no doubt got fed up with the way his gran was taking advantage of him and lashed out at her. I'm sure he didn't mean it, but he's quite a big chap. He then arranged to 'find' her body this morning. We need to tie up a few loose ends, but I'm sure that's what happened. Those detectives from the town are pretty good, but, as I told them, you can't beat local knowledge. They've been very appreciative of my insights into the murder, and this morning the senior officer on the case said that he didn't know what they'd have done without me. Yes, those were his exact words. He went on to say that he was quite unsure how best to use my particular skills."

"I can just imagine him expressing those sentiments," said Steve, whose knowledge of sarcasm was obviously far more advanced than that of the deluded constable.

"You seem to ignore the fact that Stan loved his gran," objected Georgia. "He had no idea that she was taking advantage of him, and she was the only family he had left."

"I thought she was suspected of dying yesterday between eleven and two," interjected the landlord. "And Stan was working here tidying up the cellar all morning and didn't leave until a couple of minutes to one. I remember because I said I would pay him till one, and he wanted to stay on for the extra minutes to put his time in, but I insisted he left because I knew he was eager to get up to the churchyard."

"And Georgia and I were at the church when he arrived. I'd got some bird food for his friends, and the church bell had just rung one o'clock when he turned up."

"He would've had time to go home from here and then run up to the church to establish his alibi," suggested the inept would-be detective.

"Run? You're suggesting he could have gone home from the pub, attacked his gran and then run up to the church in a matter of ten minutes at most? You're talking about someone who has to concentrate on being able to walk, let alone run," argued Georgia. "And, by the way, he was with us in the churchyard for most of the afternoon, so you can eliminate him."

"We don't rule anybody in, and we don't rule anybody out," said the would-be detective as he quoted what he had heard in so many crime thrillers on the TV, but he did so without conviction, before adding, "He was certainly acting suspiciously when I turned up there this morning. He had apparently dialled 999 and called the emergency services, but when we got there, he was just calmly sitting eating chocolate biscuits from a large tin."

"He was undoubtedly hungry and surprised to be able to get his hands on what was probably his gran's special hoard of chocolate biscuits," argued Steve as he and Georgia took their drinks out to the garden.

There was, naturally, a great deal of discussion among the customers to speculate what might have happened to Stan's gran, but it was generally believed that Stan could not have harmed her. Stan, the gentle being who cared for the creatures in the churchyard, could surely not have been capable of such violence, and the apparent timing made it impossible for him to have attacked the old woman he loved. It was generally felt that the results of the full postmortem would show that Stan could not possibly have committed the crime. The undoubted truth was that Stan was the least likely person to have attacked his gran. Georgia and Steve had bid goodnight to their friends in the garden and were on their way through the lounge bar when they saw a stranger entering the pub. There was a moment's hush in the pub as the visitor walked in. This was due to nothing more than casual inquisitiveness about the identity of the stranger rather than any overt xenophobia, and the room soon reverted to the general buzz of conversations. It was only as they left the pub that something in Georgia's memory caused her to comment.

"By Hell! The beard threw me for a while, but that was Brad Carter. The scar on his forehead was a giveaway, but what's he doing back here? He's got a nerve after what he did to Stan."

"He's probably a reformed character and may just want to settle down to being back in a place he might have called home. I guess we've got to give him a chance; life can't have been easy for him since the accident with prison and all that."

"It's not been a bed of roses for Stan either, so don't expect people in the village to accept him with open arms, and it may be more than a coincidence that he turns up in the village at the time that Martha is found injured," she declared.

"I think we have to be cautious about making such suggestions. We should leave all such speculation to our local sleuth."

"Agreed," declared Georgia. "But you have to admit that if you wanted to suspect anyone, then Brad Carter is a more likely candidate than Daft Danny's suggestion that Stan did it."

It was a few days later that Constable Bright let it be known that his 'inside knowledge' indicated that the results of the pathology examination had concluded that Martha Turner had, in fact, died of a heart attack and the injury to her head had been caused as she fell to the floor. In a bizarre way, this was good news for the village. While nobody suspected Stan could have been guilty, with the exception of PC Bright, the fact that there could have been a murderer in the village led to a lot of suspicion, and some of the inhabitants felt unsafe in their own homes if there was a killer on the loose. It was generally known that the old woman had never been popular; apart from the mean treatment of her grandson, she was seen by most as a miserable, selfish individual who never went out of her way to be civil to anyone. As the general rumours had initially gone around, many suspects were suggested who might be deemed to have had a reason to do her harm, and when it was known that Brad Carter was in the village, there were those who put him at the top of their lists.

The truth was that Martha had upset a lot of people over the years, and no one missed her, apart from Stan. Living with his gran was all he could remember, and he liked to have that consistency in his life. Despite her treatment of him, he genuinely loved her, and in the time since her death, he had seemed to be completely lost. He wandered around the village in a general state of mild confusion; he still kept up his usual routine of looking after the churchyard, but Martha had been the central stabilising factor for him, and he missed that force from his life. Although he had the freedom of the whole house now, he still spent most of the day occupying himself in the village as he had done since he came out of hospital.

He had turned up at the churchyard with the intention of digging a grave for his grandmother, but the vicar had explained that it couldn't be done immediately until the police released the body. The vicar's attempts to suggest that Stan might want someone else to do that particular job fell on deaf ears. Stan knew it was *his* graveyard, and he knew that a plot had been reserved next to his mother's. Above all, Stan wanted to do the job as a final gesture of respect for his gran.

Eventually, the medical examination having been completed, permission was given for the burial to be planned. Stan had no idea of the complexities of arranging a funeral; as far as his involvement had extended in the past, all he had ever done was dig a hole and then, after the body was lowered in and the mourners had finished at the graveside, he would discreetly fill the grave in. He prided himself on his contribution to the procedure. It was not as simple as it might appear. The grave had to have precise dimensions and was generally dug a day or so before the interment. In deference to the sensitivity of the mourners, the excavated soil would be neatly stored nearby and covered in a blanket of artificial grass, so it gave the general appearance of a grassy bank rather than cold earth. Stan referred to this structure as 'the green hill'. He had come up with this name, having frequently heard the congregation in the church celebrating the fact that "*There is a green hill far away*". Stan had no idea why that hill should be important, but he took great pride in making his look almost natural, even to the extent of arranging some artificial flowers along the edge if no fresh flowers had been provided by the mourners. Stan always took pride in his work, and he wanted to ensure that his gran's funeral would be carried out with particular care.

The undertakers were very helpful, and Colin Foreman made sure he was available to explain things. His experiences over the years with his son Mark meant that he could go through the issues with Stan in clear terms without sounding patronising. There were also one or two financial matters that needed sorting out, and Stan had no chance of being able to do all that. As there would be no relatives to inform, it was arranged to have the funeral relatively quickly, and a date was set for the following week. Tony at the pub offered to put on a few sandwiches for the wake, and Clara was called upon to do a simple wreath for the top of the coffin.

Stan still continued to spend a lot of time in the graveyard, occupying himself with what minor jobs he could find. He spent more time than usual by his mother's grave trying to remember anything about her, but it was a blank. Even the few photographs he had seen of her sparked no memories, and his gran had rarely spoken of her. He looked over the area allocated for his gran and started to make general plans in his head as to how he would go about it and, in particular, where he would store the displaced earth. It was while he was reflecting on this issue that Georgia arrived.

"Hello, Stan, I've brought a few treats up for your friends. There's a portion of quiche and some chicken skin from our dinner last night. There's also a bit of rather dry Victoria sponge, but I'm sure it will go down well."

"Thank you, Georgia. Paddy likes sweet things. It's very kind. My friends will be coming soon."

"No problem. We hate to see food going to waste, and we know how much your friends like a few treats. How are you feeling now?"

"I want to get on with Gran's plot, but I have to wait. I want to do it nice for her, next to Mum. Did you know my mum?"

"Not really. I saw her around the village now and then, but she spent a lot of time in the house with her mum when I knew her."

The fact was that Martha Turner had always been very protective with her daughter after Stan's imminent arrival had been announced, and after his accident the old lady had tightened her grip on her daughter even more, so she was rarely seen out of the house. Martha had effectively hidden her daughter away. Stan seemed satisfied to hear Georgia's meagre recollections about his mother, and he sat quietly on the bench for a while in silence.

"Steve and I wondered if you would like to go down to the pub with us this evening for a quiet drink about seven o'clock?"

"Seven? I don't know." He hesitated before declaring, "Seven, yes, seven at the pub. Be nice."

Having agreed that they would meet up at the pub, Georgia left the food for Stan's friends and went back to think about what she would do for Steve's dinner when he arrived home from his pea-packing exploits.

CHAPTER FOUR

The pub was unusually busy that evening when the couple arrived, and they approached the bar to be greeted by Monica.

"Hello, and what would you like today?"

"Two large glasses of Shiraz, please, Monica," said Steve. "It's rather busy in here tonight; is there something special on?"

"We've got a few of Mark's friends from the day centre in. Today, it's his girlfriend Celia who is celebrating her birthday, and one of the volunteer drivers has been round and collected some of the guests."

"I had no idea you had a special function on," added Georgia.

"It's not exactly the highlight of the season," explained the barmaid. "But when some of the students at the day centre have their birthdays, they like to get together, and they know they are always welcome here. It's good to see attitudes are slowly improving, but people who are 'different' aren't always accepted willingly. I'm often asked to provide some basic refreshments, and they are always well-behaved and seem to really enjoy life. It's nice to be able to offer them a bit of a chance to enjoy themselves and to socialise. Mark and Celia have been an item for years now, and it's heart-warming to see how much they enjoy each other's company. You may have observed that Mark is a bit of a flirt, but it's obvious that Celia is special to him, and she dotes on him. He frequently refers to her as his fiancée, and she loves it when he calls her that."

It was at this point that Mark rushed over, and they feared a joke was about to hit them.

"Knock knock," exclaimed the young comedian, looking at Steve.

"Who's there?" he responded dutifully.

"Na na."

"Na na who?"

"Na na your business," came the punchline with exuberant hilarity.

Mark was keen to build on the success of his act, and he turned to Georgia.

"Knock knock."

"Who's there?" she replied with a hint of trepidation.

"Olive."

"Olive who?"

"Olive you beautiful lady, my sweetheart, will you run away with me?"

It was a poor joke, and the way it drifted into Mark's usual love song didn't improve it, but he was beside himself with laughter that, as ever, was contagious. Still chuckling to himself, he wandered back to rejoin his friends, almost bumping into the individual that Georgia recognised as Brad Carter. The stranger muttered something at Mark and then made his way to the bar.

"Evening, gorgeous," he greeted Monica in a way that sounded over-familiar rather than cordial. "A large Scotch, please, darling, and have one yourself."

"No thank you, sir, I don't drink while I'm working."

"Perhaps we can have a drink when you've finished?" The suggestion was made with what he might have thought was a knowing look but which came over as an offensive leer to Monica.

"I don't fraternise with customers, sir," she said, placing his drink in front of him.

"Oh! You're a choosy one, aren't you?"

"In your case, I certainly am," she replied and turned her back on him to attend to some unimportant task on the optics. It was at this point that Stan made his entry and walked over to stand with the small group at the bar. Without knowing it, he was standing right alongside the man who had run him off the bridge that fateful night, but even if Brad hadn't grown a beard, Stan would never have recognised him as the man who ruined his life. Stan had been in hospital all through the court case, which also explained why Brad didn't know who had joined him at the bar. The potential drama within the situation struck Georgia, who wondered if Brad might have seen Stan regularly before the accident. But she calculated that Stan had been away at university for three years prior to the accident, and there was little chance of him being recognised from any time before that. While Georgia was pondering all this, Steve was seeing to the practicality of buying Stan a beer, but he had to wait for a moment as Brad had ordered another large whisky.

Stan took a sip of his pint, and the trio were about to walk over to one of the tables when Brad began to cause a bit of a scene at the bar. It was quite obvious by now that he had been drinking before he ever got to the pub, and he was not a quiet drunk.

"You're supposed to be nice to customers," he asserted in an aggressive and slightly blurred voice. "You won't take a friendly drink with me, but you make this menagerie welcome," he said, gesturing wildly towards Mark and his group.

"I think you've had enough and ought to be getting along home," asserted Monica.

"Don't think that we don't all know what you and Tony get up to in the cellar; it's common knowledge. Get rid of the customers and then head for the cellar; we know!"

Before Monica could respond, Stan turned to the drunk and looked him straight in the eye before pointing out, "You're not a nice man."

"And what are you going to do about it, big boy?"

"Nothing," came the reply, and then, after a moment's silence and with unchallengeable logic in a calm voice, he explained, "I can't make you into a nice man."

Brad didn't know what to make of this remark, and being aware of the size of Stan and the fact that he showed no signs of being intimidated, decided to back down. He left the pub, much to the relief of some of the customers who thought there was going to be a fight.

"Thanks for that, Stan. I could have handled him," explained the barmaid, "But a little bit of back-up is always appreciated. I'll put another pint in for you when you've finished that one, love."

Stan was delighted. He didn't see what he'd done as being exceptional but appreciated the offer of an extra pint. Even though he now had access to his money and could afford to go out regularly, he still had his old mindset of being prepared to look for extra jobs on the off chance of earning himself some small reward, and he saw the extra pint as a welcome bonus.

"He's an obnoxious piece of work," commented Georgia, nodding in the direction of the departed drunk.

"Yes, but we get his sort in from time to time," confided Monica with a smile before adding, "Mind you, if my sex life was anything like as energetic as he suggested, I'd be too tired to finish a shift here."

"I wonder if he's moved back permanently," said Steve. "We could certainly do without his sort causing trouble."

"Colonel Mike said he thought he saw Brad down by one of those holiday caravans on the other side of the river just beyond the bridge," said Monica. "So he may just be here for a short break. Most of the vans are taken up by people spending a few days at the nature reserve, but some are rented out on a permanent basis. Colonel Mike had been seeing to his beehives and then walked further upriver when he spotted Brad's pickup truck parked by one of the caravans, and he's pretty sure it was Brad who was wandering around it."

"Perhaps we should inform our intrepid police officer about it?" queried Georgia. "Although I expect the local bush telegraph will have got the message to him by now."

"He's one of those guys that I could take an instant dislike to," admitted Steve. "He seems incapable of saying anything without making it sound sleazy. I've met some drunks over the years and, in moderation, I can take happy drunks, boring drunks, miserable drunks and even noisy drunks, but aggressive, slimy individuals like him can spoil an evening for everybody."

"People in the trade inform me that he was always a difficult customer," confided Monica. "The night of the incident on the bridge was not the first time he was known to have created a scene at a pub and driven off after too much to drink, and he was barred from a couple of pubs in town. There was one notable occasion when Jeremy Hancock, the landlord at the Dog and Whistle, barred Carter for no apparent reason. Carter walked into the pub one evening, relatively sober, and before he could say anything, old Jeremy told him he was barred. Carter protested his innocence and asked why he was being refused service, to which the landlord replied, 'Just for being Brad Carter.' Jeremy had a powerful way with words."

Throughout this conversation, Stan had been quietly standing, sipping his drink, quite oblivious to his own tragic involvement with Brad on the bridge that night. He was enjoying a pleasant evening with friends, and his evening got even better when Mrs Simpson turned up carrying Snoopy. Stan's love of animals extended to dogs, and he gently stroked it, and the little dog seemed genuinely pleased to see him.

"Who was that horrible man?" asked the devoted dog carrier. "He almost knocked me over outside and shouted nasty things at Snoopy when I was walking him along the path. When the little darling barked at him, probably in his own brave way trying to defend me, the great oaf even tried to kick him. He was so drunk he didn't hit Snoopy, but the little mite was terrified."

"That was Brad Carter," explained Monica. "And by the look of him, he's been drinking all day. He won't be allowed in here if he starts that sort of behaviour."

"Oh, Brad Carter. Isn't he the man that…" She suddenly became aware of Stan and quickly rethought her question. "Has been away for a while?"

"One and the same, unfortunately," replied Monica. "And he's systematically going around putting everyone's backs up. His time away doesn't seem to have done him any good. He was an offensive piece of work before his 'holiday', and he's not changed much if this evening's performance is anything to go by."

Mrs Simpson and her brave little defender went over to her regular seat, and Snoopy waited for the magic mints to appear from the bag. Shortly after that, Stan walked over and sat beside them, eager to spend a bit more time with his little canine friend. Some of Mark's friends from the day centre were also drawn to the little dog and were keen to stroke him. Snoopy obliged them, but his mind was set on his mints. Georgia and Steve both remarked on the way Stan was part of the little group, and he was even seen to smile from time to time. The evening out had been a success, and by the time the couple were ready to leave, Stan was obviously having a good time, so they bid him goodnight and set off home.

"It was good to see Stan enjoying himself a bit," observed Georgia as she walked off, hand-in-hand with Steve, "but I worry about how he will cope on his own. His gran controlled his life completely. She was just a bully. I'll bet her husband was glad to get away from her."

"Her husband went for a divorce then?" asked Steve.

"No, he died, and I'm sure he only did it to get away from her. She made his life hell. It was obvious that there was no love between them, and when he died, she reverted to her maiden name and coerced her daughter into doing the same, as if to spite him. Our Martha Turner was formerly Martha Truelove, and that name certainly never suited her less-than-loving personality. If he'd still been around, then I'm sure her husband would have been the prime suspect for her 'murder', and he'd be dancing for joy now. Lately, she only had Stan to persecute. He had very little freedom, but she organised things for him, and he appreciated that. I'm convinced he did more than his fair share of the work around the house, and I know he did a lot of the routine errands, but she was the one that knew about domestic routines. She just told him what to do and never bothered to try and teach him how to cope with domestic life so he could help himself. It was convenient for her that he was dependent on her and unlikely to try and do things for himself rather than for her. Mark's dad, Colin, is being very supportive, but he's got his work cut out with Mark."

"There must be some agency that can help Stan. He's quite capable of doing a lot of routine things and could be helped to learn how to do more. At first glance, he doesn't appear to have any major problems, but he is vulnerable, and people could take advantage of him. I suspect that the house will go to him, and he has savings, so he could become a target for some unscrupulous individuals."

"Colin is working with the funeral directors, but he can't be expected to sort out all the finances," she said. "I don't know if there was a will, but if there was, then I suspect it will have been drawn up by her solicitor. I know she employed some legal representative when trying to find out about Stan's compensation. I don't want to be seen to be interfering, but someone needs to do something."

"Why don't you have a word with Mark's dad and see what you might be able to come up with in terms of support for Stan?"

"OK. I will, and there's no time like the present. Colin will be going to the pub to meet Mark soon, so we can nip back and see if we can help sort something out for Stan."

When the couple returned to the pub, it was quite a surprise to Monica, who had been joined behind the bar by Tony.

"Back again so soon; have you forgotten something?" she asked.

"We've just been thinking about Stan's position," replied Steve. "He's going to find life complicated without Martha to boss him around. He's financially better off now that she hasn't got her claws into him, but we were worried about the fact that he could be an easy target for anyone unscrupulous enough to take advantage of him. He's so trusting and expects everyone to be as genuine as he is. We wondered if Colin could suggest any way to help him as he must have some insight into the situation after looking after Mark's needs."

"You're not the only ones who are concerned about the lad," commented Tony.

"Yes," added Monica. "Quite a few of the regulars have said that they would like to help, but there is a general reluctance to be seen as interfering."

"We all want to help," added Tony. "He's a smashing chap and a useful member of the village; he does all sorts of odd jobs for people, and he does remarkably well keeping the churchyard looking good. We would all hate to see him being coerced into going off to live in some sort of care home in town. Admittedly, he does need some domestic support, and I'm sure he would be well looked after in such a place, but the village is all he knows. As far as he can recollect, his life started here when he came back from hospital, and he loves all the friends he has in the churchyard. He doesn't chat much when he's working around the pub, but when he does, it is usually about the animals up by the church. Even now, when he has a house he can stay in during the day, he prefers to spend a lot of his time at St Augustine's with his friends."

"Yes, he's so gentle with them, and his general air of calmness seems to put many of them at ease. He literally has some of them eating out of his hand, and I know he'd miss all that if he had to move away," added Steve.

"The minibus will be here just after nine to pick up the birthday gang, and Colin will be along just before that to collect Mark and to have a quick pint," explained Monica. "In the meantime, can I get you another drink?"

The young couple took no persuading, and after collecting two small glasses of red wine, they went over to take a seat by the door. As they sat and waited for Colin to turn up, they watched Mark and his group from the day centre. While they all appeared to be having a good time together, it was obvious that, for some of the time, Mark and Celia were engrossed in their own company as they sat holding hands and sharing some private conversation. Colin soon arrived, and after collecting a pint and another Vesper Martini for Mark and a coke for Celia, he left him with his friends and came over to see Georgia and Steve.

"Tony says you wanted to see me," said Colin. "Mark hasn't been annoying you, has he?"

"Not in the slightest," Georgia reassured him. "In fact, he is often the highlight of our visits down here. He's obviously so bubbly and entertaining."

"Yes," replied the older man as he glanced over at his son, who was sitting next to his girlfriend. "He likes to play up to his public, but he has his sensitive side as well. You can see how he quietens down when he's with Celia. He's been with her for over two years now, and he makes no secret of the fact that he is very keen to be with her. She positively glows when she's with him, and it causes me some concern."

"Why is that?" asked Georgia. "Surely, if they are so happy together, then that's a good thing?"

"Oh, I'm happy that they are so pleased to be together, but you may have heard that he talks of her as his fiancée; well, he's now got it into his mind that they want to get married."

"I just thought the whole fiancée thing was part of his imaginary world like his James Bond persona," commented Steve.

"His secret agent role is a bit of an imaginary life, and in a way he knows that, but he is very serious about his desire to get married, and my limited conversations with Celia suggest that she is equally committed to the idea. Mark signalled his intentions within a few months of meeting her, and at first it was easy to assume that it was just a temporary infatuation and to persuade him that it would be better to wait for a while. Frankly, I had hoped that the relationship would just fade away as most young romances do, but they are both still keen. I've known Celia's parents since our children were at school together, and recently we have talked about the relationship. If you have a child that is special, then you have a responsibility that may extend beyond that of other parents. The standard parenting model suggests that you make decisions for your children until they are capable of sorting themselves out, and then you stand back and let them get on with their lives, which includes letting them make their own mistakes. If your child has extra difficulties, then you end up controlling their lives for longer, and it can be hard to accept that at some point you may have no right to continue making those decisions even when you have grave reservations about your children making a mess of their lives. You often see them being hurt in their younger years as they face up to challenges that the rest of us don't have, and the prospect of them being hurt in an adult relationship is hard to face. I don't want to be seen as reneging on my duties as a father, but how long can I go on controlling Mark's life? Am I doing right by him?"

"I guess that I'm like many people," added Steve. "It's easy to forget that Mark is an adult; he's slightly older than me! I can't imagine how I would feel if someone told me that I couldn't live with the person I love."

"As a parent, it can be difficult to accept that your 'child' is a grown-up, and with Mark and Celia, there are other considerations. Do they know what love is? What about the possibility of children? Where would they live? These, and a hundred other questions, have been occupying my mind for a long time."

"It's a hell of a responsibility even deciding whether or not you want the responsibility," added Georgia. "Steve and I have been lucky in that my mum accepted that Steve and I want to be together, but you're right about some parents finding it hard to accept such things; Steve's parents know we are living together here, but they still have reservations about our sleeping arrangements when we visit them."

"It's interesting that you question whether or not Mark and Celia know what love is," added Steve. "You could question whether any of us know what love is. The only proof of the quality of any relationship is to try it. I've no doubt that you would hate to see either of them hurt if the relationship broke up, but do they deserve a chance? I'm sure that has been in your thoughts as well, and I'm certain that you will do what you think is best for Mark; I just don't envy you the dilemma."

"On a different, but not dissimilar topic, we wanted to have a word with you about Stan," said Georgia. "A lot of people have been saying how pleased they are to see what you are doing for him. All the complications of having to deal with a person's death are obviously beyond him, and we know you are sorting things out with the undertakers, but it is all really too much for one person to take on, particularly in the light of your current deliberations over Mark's future."

"I don't mind," said Colin. "I'm retired and have time to sort things out, but I must admit that it's very complicated. I had to deal with my wife's funeral, and that was hard enough, what with all the emotional turmoil and all, but at least I knew what our financial position had been. I have no idea what Martha's finances were like, and I don't want to be poking around her house looking to see what the financial position is for Stan. Our Mark has a very good social worker, and while we were recently discussing his 'engagement', she has agreed to look into Stan's position to see what immediate help can be given, but I've taken the liberty of saying that I don't want to see him being taken into one of the care homes in town. She seemed to think that some sort of care package could be organised, but she couldn't promise anything until after a full review of his circumstances."

"That could be a big help," added Georgia, before adding, "Nobody seems to know much about Stan's gran. She was pretty good at dishing the dirt when it came to local gossip, but her own life was pretty much a mystery. All we do know is that she loved to be in control."

"It's sad to see the way the house is divided; it's like two separate units," explained Colin. "Martha obviously had the majority of the house and certainly had a comfortable life. Stan appeared to spend all his time when he was at home in his small room upstairs or in the kitchen. I found it enlightening to note that he has no trouble operating the washing machine, but I've had to teach him how to operate the television. He informed me that he was only allowed to join her and watch the television when he had been good. He is obviously still reluctant to go into what he sees as her part of the home. She treated him more as domestic staff rather than family, and he wasn't even paid the minimum wage."

By the time Georgia and Steve left the pub, they felt slightly better, knowing that Mark's social worker might be able to make some suggestions about Stan's situation.

"It was interesting to get some insight into the issue Colin was facing with Mark's relationship with Celia," observed Steve. "It's made me realise, once again, how lucky I am to be with you. The relative normality in the way our love developed is something that Mark and Celia have so far been denied. The domestic relationships at university were originally challenging for a burgeoning romance, and my parents' attitude was less than helpful, but Mark and Celia would appear to have no time to be together, so how can they ever find out what their love means?"

CHAPTER FIVE

The next Sunday afternoon, the cricket team had what was classed as an away game against a team from the White Horse in Uxford, so Steve was surprised to hear that it was to be played on the Hartbridge pitch. Don had explained that this was not unusual as some of the local teams did not have their own pitches, and the facilities at Hartbridge were particularly good. This was not unrelated to the fact that the Trout Inn was conveniently situated near the pitch, and the pub was pleased to do the catering at a very reasonable price. This particular fixture was to have been played on the village green in Uxford, but due to a mix-up, the green was to be in use for a classic car rally. When the team did arrive, it was obvious that one or two of them had taken the opportunity of having a pre-match tipple at the White Horse before setting out. The landlord of that particular hostelry was a fervent supporter of the team, and on match days he would secretly permit the team members and supporters to come in early and have a pre-match pint or two to settle their nerves. One or two of the players had been at the pub for ten o'clock, and it would be fair to say that their pre-match nerves had been well and truly settled.

While such illicit drinking was good for business at the pub, it did little for the subsequent match, and this largely accounted for the poor results that the White Horse team posted throughout the season. They had never actually won a match, but they did manage a draw one day when the match was rained off. They were, however, generally acknowledged as the team who always seemed to enjoy their games. When they arrived in their various cars, they had the general appearance of a group preparing to enjoy a pub day out to Blackpool rather than a team of finely honed athletes about to play a cricket match. Bill Norton was obviously annoyed at the thought that anyone could approach a game of cricket with such a disrespectful attitude but resisted the temptation to say anything.

The long dry spell of weather that the area had enjoyed was due to end, but when the teams collected before the match the forecast heavy rains had not arrived. The sky was cloudy, and Bill Norton, in his pre-match gathering with his men, was keen to point out that the conditions would favour the 'swing' bowlers. Some of the team members sagely nodded their agreement with this assessment, although there was a general recognition of the fact that they didn't have a bowler who would claim to have the necessary skills to produce such a delivery.

Hartbridge batted first and, against the most inept bowlers and a dismal display of fielding, they quickly amassed two hundred and fifty runs and only lost one wicket. Bill was imperious as he hit a hundred and sixty not out; he was determined to take his hallowed game seriously even if the opposition weren't. After the White Horse team lost their first six batsmen for only thirty runs, Bill felt he could risk giving his new team member a chance to bowl, and the ball was thrown to Steve, who promptly went on to take two wickets in his over without conceding a run. Bill stepped up to bowl the next over and finished off the opposing batsmen just in time as the heavens opened. The players and the smattering of spectators scattered for cover. The game had been convincingly won, but Bill was less than satisfied with the day. In his eyes, although Hartbridge had won, cricket had lost. In the bar afterwards, Georgia greeted Steve.

"Well done, darling. I'm no cricket expert, but I thought your bowling was very impressive."

"Thanks," he said before looking around to ensure that none of the White Horse players were within earshot and then continuing. "Frankly, given the way they were playing, your mother could probably have bowled them out."

"You were lucky to finish before the storm blew in; just look at it," she declared, pointing to the rain pelting onto the windows. "We're going to get absolutely soaked on the way home unless this lot eases off a bit."

The pub was often quite full on a Sunday afternoon after a cricket match, but it was even more so today as those customers who had been in the habit of drinking in the garden had opted for the shelter of the bar. Both the teams were enjoying a convivial post-match drink together as it had never been a bitterly fought game. The White Horse team never engaged in any 'needle' match and were gracious losers, which was not surprising as they'd had countless seasons of practice in that role. Georgia looked around the room to see who had turned up. She was delighted to see that Stan had decided to put in an appearance, and she saw that he was talking to Mike Colly. The two men got on quite well, and she had seen them together quite recently sitting in the churchyard. It appeared that when Mike went along to check on his beehives, he would nip into the churchyard and chat with Stan if he was there. They seemed an unlikely couple; the gently spoken, naïve young man and the weathered ex-soldier who had seen a lot of the world. They had certain things in common in that they were both tall, well-built men with a taciturn disposition that meant they could spend quite a lot of time together, during which neither man spoke very much, but they both appeared comfortable with that.

Colin was there with Mark, who was strangely quiet until he saw Georgia, and he quickly made his way over to see her. Even before he got to her, he went into his routine.

"Hello, lovely lady, my sweetheart," came the familiar greeting. "What has one wheel and flies?"

Georgia looked to Steve for inspiration but then admitted defeat.

"A wheelbarrow full of dung!" The very mention of the word dung seemed to make this recent joke particularly funny to Mark, and he was still laughing when Brad Carter walked past on his way to the bar.

"I don't like that nasty man," confided Mark, looking towards the newcomer. "He calls me names, and he's rough. Why doesn't he go away?"

"There are a lot of people who wish he'd go away, Mark," admitted Steve. "But sometimes we have to just put up with horrible people."

"James Bond could make him go away," said the young would-be secret agent, pointing an imaginary gun at Brad's back.

"Nice thought, Mark, but it isn't always that easy," explained Georgia.

For the next hour, the couple sat together quietly, talking as young lovers do about their plans for a future together. The rain continued to cascade down in almost biblical proportions, but the young couple were happy and dry inside the pub. Apart from the weather, it had all the makings of a very pleasant day. But the relative calm of the pub was shattered by a very noisy disturbance at the bar, and the whole pub was treated to an escalating confrontation involving Brad Carter, who had obviously been steadily drinking his way through a considerable amount of whisky. The room fell silent to listen to what was going on.

"That's it!" announced the landlord, addressing his remarks to Brad Carter in a voice that rang out clearly around the bar. "You're barred. Now get out."

A spontaneous cheer erupted from the assembled customers, which only served to enrage Brad.

"I've got my rights. You can't do that," argued the drunk.

It was at this point in the mini-drama that Mike Colly faced up to Carter and, in a very calm but strangely threatening way, gave his slant on the situation.

"That's where you're wrong, sunshine. Tony has every right to throw you out; he's got the law on his side, and I've got every right to throw you out because I've got muscle on my side, and if you don't remove yourself from these premises, I shall exercise my rights by marching you to the door over there and throwing you out. I reckon I could throw you as far as the middle of the road if you want me to try."

Brad could see he had no option but to comply with the landlord's instruction. As he staggered to the door, the assorted cricket players led the jeering, causing the drunk to pause and try to retaliate for this verbal onslaught.

"You lot of losers, dressed up like big kids in your poncy white clothes. Why don't you grow up and find something useful to do with your weekends?"

This weak attempt at trying to goad the collected sportsmen only caused even more hilarity among them as they all raised an index finger, like a gang of merry umpires delivering their verdicts, and chanted, "Out, out, out," in unison. So the shamed drunk had no option but to heed their chant and leave, only to be faced by the continuing downpour. He was a pathetic figure as he stumbled off along the road, cursing wildly to himself, but he would get no sympathy from the crowds in the pub.

While all this was going on, Mike Colly had quietly turned back to the bar and continued with his evening as though nothing had happened. When Steve went over to get more drinks for himself and Georgia, he couldn't resist the temptation to try and find out what had happened to cause the uproar.

"It's my fault," claimed Tony, "I should have barred him earlier, but today he has been particularly offensive. He was pestering young Karen earlier. She came in for a drink and to watch her friend who was in the team, and Brad started his smutty chat-up lines. It is a sad reflection of our times that Karen is probably quite capable of coping with mild lechery, but he was coming on strong, and Monica had to warn him to behave. As his whisky intake increased, he got worse, so she asked him to leave, but he wouldn't go, claiming that we couldn't expect him to leave in this weather. I came up at that point and informed him that he would have to go and it wouldn't matter if it had been blowing a blizzard with ten degrees of frost. It was then that he really started. He went on about the fact that we accepted all sorts of oddballs in here and referred to the group who had been in from the day centre with Mark, and he made a remark about Stan not being 'normal'. I noticed that this had hit a nerve with Colonel Mike, who turned slowly to face the slime ball and it was at that point that I decided to bar Brad permanently, if only for his own safety, and you saw what happened."

"I can assure you," observed Steve, "that we are all glad to see the back of him and thanks to you for your intervention, Mike."

"Yes, thanks, Mike," said Tony. "Officially, I should inform you that we can't have you threatening another customer with violence, but personally, I think you were just expressing a sentiment that we would all endorse."

Mike smiled gently and then returned to his conversation with Stan, who had thankfully been oblivious to the comments made by the drunk.

"In the short time he's been back, the offensive Mr Carter has managed to offend nearly everybody in the village. It's almost as though he's on a mission to do so," said Tony. "If he could keep off the drink, it might help, but he still seems to resent going to prison for what he thought was just a bit of an accident. He's probably a reasonable guy when he's sober, but he rarely seems to be so. On top of that, he still drives that damn great truck of his around, and I'm pretty sure that his blood-alcohol levels are rarely low enough for him to pass a breath test. It's a good job he didn't have the vehicle with him today, or he would definitely have driven rather than get wet."

"Yes, I've seen him driving around occasionally," added Steve. "Most of the time he crawls around as if he's aware he has to be extra cautious. It's interesting that so many people who have had too much to drink think that they will be OK if they drive very slowly and concentrate on looking sober, as if that will compensate for the fact that their reaction times are shot at. In Carter's case, he does sometimes belt along the High Street like the idiot he is."

"I've been hearing all sorts from customers when they've been in here, and none of them have a good word for Carter. I met Hannah Cordwell at the wholesalers, and she was telling me that he goes into her shop every day to buy his whisky. She admits that she knows she should refuse to serve him, but she's intimidated by him, and young Karen can't seem to be able to refuse him his booze."

"What does he do all day?" asked Steve. "I'm not around the village much during the week, but he always seems to be wandering around, and he stinks of whisky all the time."

"He doesn't appear to have a job. Mrs Holland, at the post office, says he goes in there frequently and withdraws cash. She heard a rumour that his mother had died and he'd inherited a bit of money that way. She's usually pretty well-informed. She seems to think that he sold the little place she had in Callerthorpe and bought one of those large caravans down by the river."

"So it's unlikely that he will be moving on," said Steve despondently. "We had hoped it was just a holiday let and that he might move on like some nomadic menace."

Steve took the drinks he had purchased back to Georgia and updated her on the sorry saga of Brad Carter. They sat as long as they could to see if the rain would stop, but it continued relentlessly, and eventually they had to risk the short run to their flat. As they stood in the flower shop, shaking some of the water from their hair and clothes, Steve laughed.

"Did anyone ever tell you that you look ravishing in that bedraggled state?" he asked.

"Did anyone ever tell you that you are weird?" she replied.

CHAPTER SIX

The fact that Don was giving him a lift to work meant that Steve no longer needed to be up at quite such an early hour so he had the opportunity to enjoy a simple breakfast with Georgia the next day. He looked out of the window and was pleased to see that it had stopped raining, but some of the heavy overnight rain was still running down the road to the nearest drainage gully.

"Did you hear that racket last night?" he asked her as he was pouring the tea.

"I thought I did, but the wind howling around made it difficult to make out what it was. It sounded like a big van or a lorry roaring down the road."

"That's what I thought," he agreed. "And then, whatever it was seemed to come back and head towards the bridge."

"It could have been some emergency vehicles. The river will be very full after all that rain, and someone might have wanted to see how the bridge was coping or to check on the river bank. The river often spills over in flood conditions, and the rain was pretty heavy for most of the afternoon and well into the night. It's strange, though, it usually takes a good twenty-four hours for the excess water to make its way down here from the high ground upriver."

"No doubt we'll hear on the grapevine in due course," he concluded before giving her a kiss and wandering out to wait for his lift. Don was on time, and the main conversation during their run into work was the amount of rain that had fallen overnight. He was apologetic about the fact that the rain had made its way in through the car's sunroof, necessitating Steve having to sit on a large plastic bag to protect him from a rather damp seat.

"The sunroof has always been a bit of a problem, and I get the odd drip of water coming through as the drainage channels don't cope too well, but the rain in the last 24 hours has just proved too much."

The journey to the factory was eventful as there were large pools of water along many stretches of the narrow country lanes. It was impossible to steer a course between them, and so the car ploughed on, throwing up waves of water onto the verges, making their journey more like a cruise than their usual daily commute. Steve was eager to point out that the minor inconvenience of sitting on a large plastic bag was still infinitely preferable to his previous experience on the bus to work. Much as he loved the bus journey through the many small villages, travelling with Don meant that it shortened his time away from home and Georgia. At university and in their time together in the holidays, Steve had always spent a large part of his time with Georgia, and he did somewhat resent being away from her. He reflected on this as they travelled home that evening but realised that when they both moved into 'proper' jobs, they would probably see less of each other. They had been spoiled over the last few years, being able to spend much of their time together, and he felt a tinge of sadness at the prospect of future employment forcing them to spend less time together. It was this thought that compelled him to greet Georgia in the shop with a lengthy, affectionate kiss. This particular impulsive gesture was a slight surprise for Georgia, just as it was for Rita, who emerged from the store room at this time to find the couple locked in an embrace.

"Sorry to interrupt," said Rita, "but I can always leave the tidying up if you're busy."

"Don't mind him," explained Georgia with a little laugh, "I think he's been getting a little too much roughage in his diet."

"I think I'll have to get my Larry to take more roughage," muttered Rita with a meaningful sigh as she said goodbye to the young couple and discreetly turned the sign on the door to signify that the shop was closed as she left to go home.

When Georgia had disentwined herself from a very welcome if somewhat unexpected embrace, she was eager to update him on the local news, and when they got up to the flat, she was quick to tell him of the day's events.

"It seems that someone has made a right mess of the cricket pitch," she announced. "Rita was telling me that Hannah, at the shop, had told her about it. Apparently, someone had driven all over the centre of the wicket. After all that rain, the ground was so soft that it was all churned up. Mrs Holland in the post office said she heard something during the night, and she'd looked out over towards the playing fields. She saw a large vehicle driving out of the park, but she couldn't be sure who it was because the vehicle had no lights on, and visibility was poor due to the horrendous rain. She was pretty sure it was a pickup like the one Brad Carter drove, but she couldn't swear to it. She spoke to Daft Danny Bright, and he seems to think it will be easy to prove it was Carter."

"Admittedly, Carter seems to be the obvious culprit after his performance in the pub last night. He was absolutely fuming with rage and fully fuelled with whisky when he left, but you have to doubt if Daft Danny could prove anything."

"There is some hope that the video security camera outside the post office might have picked up something, and Danny has taken the recording away to see if it helps, but it's hardly a major crime that will take priority over other things going on in the county," she said.

"Admittedly, but it will be regarded as an extremely big crime by Bill at the cricket club," explained Steve. "He's poured his efforts into the club for years and it has a deserved reputation as one of the best-equipped ones in the area. The wicket wasn't exactly up to county level, but it's taken him years to get it into the condition it was in. He will be shattered by the news, and then he'll want blood. Ruining his ground will be seen as sacrilege and justification for bringing back capital punishment. If it's as bad as it sounds, it will take him weeks to get the wicket into a barely playable state, and Bill will have missed some of his precious cricket season. There's only a couple of matches left, but we'll miss those unless he can negotiate alternative venues."

"I've never known anybody who could annoy as many people in such a short time," declared Georgia. "He is gradually drinking himself to death and he seems to want to blame everyone else for the position he's in. I gather, from reports of the trial in the local paper, that he even tried to claim that Stan had suddenly thrown himself in front of the car. All the evidence showed that he was lying, and the jury saw through it, but he never accepted any of the blame and showed no remorse then or since."

Their conversation was interrupted by the sound of the doorbell, and Steve went down to open the front door only to find Clara there.

"Why didn't you just let yourself in, Daisy?" he asked.

"During the working day, I would use my key to get into the shop, but I have to respect that this is your home, and I'm not so old as to have forgotten that young people sometimes prefer not to be disturbed in the evening. I also met Rita on the way here, and she suggested that you might be busy."

"I take your point, and thanks," he said, smiling. "Anyway, go straight up, we are receiving visitors."

"I just wondered how you were getting on," explained Clara. "Ed and I are hoping to get away for a few days, and I just wanted to check everything was alright with the shop and all."

"You mean you just wanted to get up to date with the gossip after the pitch incident last night, Mum."

"I must admit to a little curiosity as to how things are going. I heard that horrible Brad creature has been particularly offensive. Hannah Cardwell tells me that he has been making a nuisance of himself at the shop and pestering Karen, so much so that her dad is threatening to go round to Carter's caravan and push it into the river, and he's got the tractor and the nerve to do just that. Apparently, Carter goes into the shop most mornings and buys a half bottle of whisky, and this morning he did so and then went and sat on the bench near the bus stop, just staring over at the playing fields with a smug smile on his face. It's as if he's taunting people after his excursion onto the cricket pitch."

"His *alleged* drive over the cricket area," corrected Steve. "But we all know that he is the one who must have done it. It was a petty, vindictive act and quite in keeping with all we've learned about the rat."

"Mrs Holland at the post office is certain it was Carter's pickup that she saw driving out of the park last night," suggested Clara. "But we'll have to see if the video records show up if it was his vehicle. To be fair, the rain was absolutely belting down and some of those security cameras are a bit indistinct at the best of times. Our less-than-wonderful local police officer says that they can take mud samples from Carter's vehicle and send them off for forensic testing in the lab to see if they match up with the cricket pitch, but I can't see the police trying to justify such time and expense to investigate an act of vandalism. Bless him, Daft Danny did go up to take mud samples from the pickup, and that may make Carter think the whole thing is being taken seriously by the police."

"I guess that PC Bright is the nearest thing we have to a deterrent, but I can't see him having much effect on Carter; he's had numerous run-ins with the law," suggested Georgia.

"When I was chatting with Hannah in the shop, she said that even Colin Foreman had been very outspoken about the way Mark has been treated by Carter. Sadly, Colin is used to people finding it hard to accept Mark and his friends, but when he heard about Carter's blatant hostility to the group in the pub, he was furious. Colin is an easy-going chap, and he's learned not to become too outspoken when people may appear insensitive, but he would have loved the opportunity to have been there in the pub to make his feelings known to Carter, and it's hard to imagine anyone in the village not feeling the same way."

Having thus updated Georgia on the situation with Carter, Clara went on to impart some new information.

"I'm not sure how true it is, but it appears that while trying to sort out some of Martha Turner's paperwork for Stan, Colin found an insurance policy she had taken out on her own life to cover funeral costs. At first, it seemed strange that she should be putting money aside to make money available for Stan, but, on reflection, she just wanted to make sure she got a fancy send-off. She was trying to impress the village even when she wouldn't be around to see her wealth being flaunted. She's going to be a bit disappointed, though, the funeral has all been arranged for next week, and Colin has already made it clear to the funeral directors that Stan wants a simple ceremony. So, if she was expecting to be in an ornate casket in a black carriage pulled by six matching horses with plumes on their heads, she is going to be disappointed. It seems that all Stan wanted was a very simple ceremony where his gran could be interred in a grave he had dug for her himself. It's rather touching to see how much he misses her despite the way she treated him. He spends a lot of time up by what will be her grave. He doesn't seem depressed in any way, but he just wants to have that tenuous connection with her. As far as I'm aware, he hasn't been to the chapel of rest to see Martha, preferring to think of her as he sits in the natural setting outdoors. When you look back at the way Martha behaved, it's hardly surprising that people believed that someone had been prepared to murder her. I don't think that Daft Danny ever accepted that it was just a natural death. He has been heard saying as much. He never mentions exactly who he thinks the 'killer' might be, but he has been seen to give what he thinks is a 'knowing look' while maintaining that he can't divulge police information. That's a laugh; in terms of local gossip, he's the biggest blabbermouth in the area."

"Yes," agreed Steve, "I think our super sleuth of a police constable saw it as an opportunity to make a name for himself by 'solving' a crime that never happened."

"I saw Stan digging a new grave when I went over to take some bits of food over for his friends this morning," said Georgia. "He seemed pleased that the ground set aside for his gran is not too full of stones, and he was making good progress, but he was ready for a break when I arrived, and we sat for a while as he threw down some bits of crisped-up chicken skin for his friends. The rooks were down very quickly, and Stan chatted to them, encouraging them not to be greedy and to leave some for the others, but they just ignored him and filled their beaks with the little delicacies before flying off. He seemed so content, sitting there and smiling. His friend Paddy managed to grab a few bits of chicken skin, and when the others had flown off, he hung around. Stan told him that there was no special treat and instructed him to come back later. The jackdaw appeared to understand and flew off to the top of one of the bigger trees and waited. His departure was obviously coincidental, but it looked like he had heeded Stan's advice. Stan didn't sit for long, and after a while he put on his gloves and quietly returned to his task."

When Rita arrived the following morning, she brought news of another incident that was occupying the minds of some of the villagers she had met on her way to work.

"Everyone's talking about the break-in at the pub," she blurted out as she took off her coat and put on her work tabard. "The big window at the back of the pub that looks out onto the garden has been smashed into a thousand pieces; glass all over the floor. I don't know what has been stolen, but Danny Bright was apparently looking into it."

"He'll soon sort it out," added Georgia, with more than a trace of sarcasm in her voice.

"It must have happened late last night, but neither Mrs Holland at the post office nor Hannah at the shop heard anything. I suppose somebody could have driven up to the pub, but Hannah is a very light sleeper, and after the cricket pitch incident she's been aware of any unusual sounds."

Throughout the day, as people came into the shop, Georgia received a number of updates about the incident at the pub, so when Steve came home she could inform him of what appeared to have gone on during the previous night.

"The initial reports of a break-in were incorrect," she stated. "It seems that someone just smashed the glass with a brick and then probably took off along the riverbank; hence there was no sound of a vehicle. No one was hurt, and nothing was stolen, but it's caused a huge amount of damage."

"I hate to jump to conclusions, but that sounds very much like Brad Carter has been up to his tricks again. He could have scarpered off down the river bank to the bridge and back to his caravan. He would have been taking his life in his hands sneaking off down that track along the riverbank in the dark, and particularly because he would undoubtedly be drunk at the time. If, as you suggested, the river will be particularly full at the moment, it's a wonder he didn't topple in and do us all a favour."

"He had been seen in the afternoon down by the bridge," added Georgia. "Mike Colly saw him leaning against the parapet when he went down to check on the hives. He was obviously quite drunk, even at that time. He was just lounging there, taking sips of whisky from his bottle and looking down at the river. Mike stood for a while watching the inebriate from a distance as he stood up and swayed. Mike said that he was willing Brad to fall over the parapet into the fast-flowing waters. In his professional days, it would no doubt have been easy to give him a quick blow to the head and throw him into the gorged river. The body would have been ten miles downstream in a few hours, and the whole village would probably have been delighted. I know that seems heartless, but the man was evil."

"So what has Daft Danny done about it?" asked Steve.

"I'm told he went straight to the caravan park to see what Brad had to say for himself, but despite repeatedly knocking loudly on the door, he couldn't get a response. After the amount of whisky he appears to have gone through, he's probably got one hell of a hangover and wouldn't be able to spring out of bed, even if he felt inclined to."

"Something will have to be done about Carter. He's on a one-man vandalism spree, and there's no telling what his warped little mind will come up with next. In the good old days, the villagers would have risen up and formed a vigilante group to drive him out. There would be no shortage of people to chase him out of the village, as he seems to have offended or insulted everyone, but it's not that easy these days. Was Mike the last one to have a sighting of Brad?" he asked.

"Karen said he went into the shop at about six o'clock. He went to get a ready meal and another small bottle of whisky. She had been told not to serve him if he was drunk, but she was obviously intimidated by the offensive article and sold him the whisky just to get him out of the shop. She thought he was heading home when he left, but frankly I don't think she cared as long as he was gone. There was no definite sighting of him after that, and I think most of us hoped that he had decided to move away, but Sherlock Bright noticed that the pickup was still parked by the side of the caravan when he called to try and interview the alleged hooligan. So it looks like it will be a waiting game to see when he emerges from his drunken slumber."

It had been yet another eventful day, so Georgia and Steve decided to go for a quick drink at the Trout Inn. The pub had slightly more customers than usual as many people had possibly turned up to get the very latest on the damage to the building. All seemed very much the same, apart from the fact that the large window at the back had been temporarily boarded over.

"Someone's made a right mess of that, Tony," said Steve, gesturing to the boarded window.

"And it's pretty obvious who was responsible," suggested the landlord. "And I'm convinced the little weasel will be brought to justice by our own redoubtable PC Bright, just as I'm certain that Christmas Day will fall in September this year."

"I'm sure we all share your confidence in the detective qualities of Daft Danny. Remember how he had convinced himself that Martha Turner had been brutally murdered and, without a shred of evidence to prove it, he started his own little investigation. He's about as competent as Inspector Clouseau. I bet his colleagues at the station took the mickey out of him after it was shown to be an accidental death and that Danny's local knowledge was proven to be absolutely worthless, as usual. At least he's unlikely to press for a team of fellow officers to be drafted in to sort this latest bout of incidents out. I suspect that he's lost what little professional credibility he might ever have had."

"On the grand scale of things, a churned-up cricket pitch and a broken window are admittedly trivial," commented Tony. "But they are still important to those of us who are affected. That wicket was Bill's pride and joy, and it took years for him to build the reputation of the cricket club. The guy was almost in tears when he first saw what had been done, and then he became incandescent with rage. He would have beaten Brad to a pulp with a cricket bat and not regretted it. The window back there has no sentimental value, but it's caused a lot of disruption. We had to clear up all the broken glass and get that temporary board put up before we could open the pub up again, and I've yet to sort out a claim on the insurance."

"There is one other disturbing factor," added Georgia. "Where is Carter likely to strike next? He seems to have got it in for the entire village. He hasn't been here long, and he's annoyed half the inhabitants already. He even had that confrontation with Stan. Fortunately, Stan's the most placid individual you could hope to meet, and it came to nothing. Brad just couldn't seem to understand Stan's passive resistance, but the little rat was obviously reluctant to mix it up with a guy of Stan's stature. The incident with Colonel Mike could have been worse, but Mike's self-control meant that ended relatively peacefully, which obviously disappointed many of the customers who would have loved to see Carter ejected onto the street. I guess that the humiliation he suffered was probably the trigger that set him off on his trail of vandalism."

"He looked a pathetic sight as he tottered down the road in that torrential rain, probably uttering obscenities aimed at the entire village," observed Steve, "I know that we mustn't jump to conclusions, but it's hard to think who else could have done it. Unless it's some master plan by Daft Danny to create a mini crime spree so that he can solve it by pinning it on someone else."

"I rather think you are overestimating Constable Bright's intellectual capacity, love," commented Georgia. "If he was the master criminal behind all this, then, after days of futile investigations, he would probably go on to arrest himself. It's about the only scenario where he could ever bring anyone to justice."

"I'm a bit surprised that Carter hasn't risked turning up here tonight to gloat over his impact on my interior renovations," added Tony. "Even though he's barred, the brazen little reprobate is just daft enough to try and get in."

"There haven't been any reports of his whereabouts at all today. We can usually keep up with any gossip in the flower shop, but nobody has mentioned seeing him, which is strange in itself as everyone is keen to follow the next chapter in the story of Dirty Dan. I think that the entire village is holding its breath, wondering where and when the next attack will be made. I guess it's too much to hope that he's left."

"A couple of the customers earlier were disappointed to report that they had seen Carter's pickup still parked outside his caravan, so it's unlikely that he's left. No doubt he will be out and about soon, causing havoc. It surely can't take him that long to sober up, but if he is around later tonight, I shall be waiting to greet him. I'm going to settle down in the bar here on a camp bed, fully clothed, and I'll be out like a shot if I hear anything strange going on. I can't promise that I will be able to show Mike's restraint either."

It was at this point that the pub was treated to Mark's entry. The moment he saw the boarded-up window, he went over and studied it carefully.

"The window's broken," he announced. "Must have been that nasty man."

"There you are," exclaimed Tony. "Even Mark knows who must have done it."

After his lengthy examination of the window and search for clues, Mark approached the group at the bar.

"Hello beautiful lady, my sweetheart," he started, but then, as if suddenly remembering something, he asked, "What does one snowman say to another?"

As usual, Georgia had no idea and reluctantly admitted as much.

"Can you smell carrot?" came the apparently hilarious answer.

"Some ill-advised individual once bought him a book with a collection of Christmas cracker jokes," explained Tony. "And from time to time, we all get to suffer them. At some point, you will no doubt be treated to the classic; what does Santa do with his fat elves? And the answer, of course, is: he sends them to an elf farm."

"No offence, Tony," commented Georgia. "But I suspect Mark's delivery of that little horror would have been better than yours."

"I guess I don't have his stage presence or his way with you women," admitted Tony.

CHAPTER SEVEN

When Rita turned up at the flower shop the next day, she was almost disappointed to have to announce that there had been no further incidents of vandalism reported in the village. She had been surprised to see Tony in the post office so early in the morning, as the nature of his work in the pub meant that he was not usually an early riser. He explained that he had been on guard in the bar overnight, and the camp bed had not been very comfortable, so his sleep had been periodically broken each time he tried to turn over. It got so bad that just after dawn he had been unable to get back to sleep, so he had decided to get up. Having walked around the pub and gardens to make sure that nothing had been disturbed, he had found time to patrol around the recreation grounds where everything seemed to be unchanged from the previous day.

"The trouble is," explained Rita, "everybody seems to be waiting to see what's going to happen next. It's naturally assumed that Carter is to blame, but no one has seen him for a while, and there's a real feeling of apprehension as to what he will get up to next. Even old Mrs Simpson has got it into her head that little Snoopy could be kidnapped by Carter, and she's only going out for brief walks and has declared her reluctance to go to the pub in case they run into him again."

"I know what you mean," agreed Georgia. "Part of the problem is that he has had run-ins with so many people that it's difficult to predict who his next target might be and what he might do to 'avenge' himself."

"Mrs Holland at the post office said she was going to have a word with Danny Bright to get him to go and confront Carter in the hope that it might dissuade him from trying anything else. Not that anyone seriously believes that he will be frightened off by knowing that PC Danny is on the case. No doubt he will be keen to be seen playing at policeman, but he doesn't inspire confidence."

"I only hope Carter doesn't decide to upset Stan," added Georgia. "They did have that little incident in the bar when Stan faced up to him, and he would be an easy target."

"And I've been told that Mark and his friends seemed to annoy Carter with their presence in the pub. He might well have assumed that their hilarity was at his expense and want to get back at them somehow. Apparently, Colin was heard arguing with Carter about his attitude to Mark and his friends, so that could put him on a list of potential targets as well. I suppose we might just be worrying needlessly, and when Carter realises how he's not wanted, he might move on again."

"I don't think he's the type to be concerned that nobody likes him," suggested Georgia. "He seems to revel in the feeling of being a victim of circumstances; it's Brad Carter against the world, as far as he's concerned."

It was a quiet morning in the shop, so Georgia took the opportunity to sort out some paperwork. There were a couple of invoices that needed to be sent off, so Rita offered to nip to the post box with them. Georgia was not at all surprised to hear that Rita had taken the opportunity to pop into the post office, ostensibly to get some stamps but mainly to catch up on village news.

"You'll never guess what's happened now," announced Rita as soon as she got back to the shop. "Danny says that Carter's caravan is empty, and there's no sign of him."

"So, has he left now?"

"It seems unclear what has happened. Danny went up to confront Carter and banged on the door again, but there was no answer. He went over to the pickup, which hadn't moved. He checked the back, but there was nothing in there, so he peered into the truck cab, which was also empty. He tried banging on the door of the caravan again, but still no reply. As Danny put it, 'having reason to fear for the safety of the occupant', he tried the door and found it to be unlocked. A quick glance inside showed there was no one present, so he called it in on his radio to report a missing person. Needless to say, the local station didn't rush to send out dozens of officers. Danny's previous attempts to create a drama over Martha Turner's 'murder' had done little to promote his image as an investigating officer, so the incident was routinely logged. Danny at least had the good sense to contact the manager of the caravan park, who had a key to Carter's caravan, which he locked before promising to inform the police if Carter returned."

"That's intriguing," mused Georgia. "So where could he have gone to? If he hasn't got his van, I suppose he could have walked, but he wasn't exactly the fittest of people. Perhaps he went towards Callerthorpe to find a different pub, having been barred from the Trout, but that's a hell of a walk, and I've no doubt that, despite his previous experiences, he would have been tempted to drive. Mike Colly saw him on the bridge teetering about, so he might have fallen in the river, and the excess water flowing down after the rain would have taken him miles. Even the strongest of swimmers would have been lucky to survive, and Carter was hardly that, and I can't imagine that there would have been hordes of people rushing to save him."

Brad Carter's whereabouts remained a subject of conversation, and the general view was that his absence from the village was something to be welcomed, especially as the following day was to be Martha Turner's funeral and the prospect of a drunk spoiling the occasion had been a matter of some concern to many. The service was due to start in Saint Augustine's at midday, and Steve, who had taken the day off to support Stan rather than out of any respect for Martha, was at the church with Georgia by half past eleven. They were not surprised to see that Stan was already there, sitting on his favourite bench. His appearance in a suit seemed so unlike him, but he was obviously intent on doing things properly for his gran. After exchanging brief greetings, the three of them sat quietly together on the bench for a while before Stan broke the silence.

"I've fed my friends. They came to see how I was. I've never done this before, but I put my suit on like Colin said. Have to be smart for Gran. She can't see me, but she'll know. I wish she was still here."

It was at this point that Georgia noticed that Stan was wearing his heavy work boots, and her gaze encouraged him to look down.

"Oh!" he said, "I forgot my smart shoes. I'll get them."

"Will you have time to get home to get them, or do you want me to run down and get them from your house?" suggested Steve.

"They're in my shed with my other clothes," answered Stan in a matter-of-fact way. "I can't work in this suit."

"So you came down this morning and changed in the shed?" asked Georgia incredulously.

"No. I was here all night. It's quiet here at night. It's not right without Gran in the house. I can think here, with my friends. I had to make sure Gran's place was ready for her." He sat looking out over the graveyard with the young couple, wiped a tear from his eye and glancing over at the grave, he continued, "It's all prepared now. She won't be disturbed, and I'll cover her up properly later when it's quiet. That's what I do."

"You're surely not going to do that yourself, Stan. You'll miss the do at the pub," observed Steve.

"She would want me to finish off her grave properly, I'm family."

Steve exchanged a few words with Georgia before making a suggestion.

"Your friends at the pub would like to see you afterwards. Why don't I run back after the service and get into some old clothes so I can help? It would only take me a couple of minutes to nip across the road, and after the job is finished and you feel it's right, we could both get down to the pub and catch some of the wake. Your friends would really want to see you."

Stan thought for a considerable time, weighing up the situation, as he watched a few large birds flying high above the churchyard with their harsh kaah calls disturbing the quietness of the morning. Eventually, he came up with a question.

"My friends would want to see me at the pub?"

"Yes, Stan," answered Georgia. "We all know how much you wanted to see to your gran's funeral, but I'm sure that she wouldn't want you to miss a chance to have a quiet drink with your friends to celebrate her life. That's what people do after funerals; they share stories of what a lovely person they have just buried. It's what people do."

The suggestion that anyone in the village would have any happy memories to share about Martha was being less than honest, but Georgia felt justified in stretching the truth.

"I've never been to a funeral before," confessed Stan, "I just prepare the grave and make sure it's left looking smart afterwards. Do you think I should go down to the pub? Would Gran have wanted that?"

"Without a doubt, Stan," she lied. "Anyway, you'd better go and change into your other shoes for the service. I don't know what you've been doing, but your boots are caked in mud. The vicar wouldn't be pleased if you took all that into the church."

"Even your friends up there are calling you to go," said Steve, looking up at the circling rooks.

"And you'll help me, Steve?"

"Of course, Stan. Now go and change your shoes before the first of your guests turn up."

It was a quarter to twelve when the mourners started to appear at the church, and they stood around awkwardly making small talk as they waited for someone to inform them what to do next. It was an unusual gathering as there were no relatives, but a sizeable number of people from the village had come along to offer support for Stan. It occurred to Georgia that none of them would have pretended that they had come because of any friendship links with Martha, but then, the less-than-dear departed would be completely oblivious as to who was there and why. Attending a funeral is a way of giving support to the deceased's family and friends, and Stan was quite overwhelmed by the number of people who had turned up. A representative from the undertakers ushered the guests into the church to take up their seats. Stan was clearly bemused by the fact that he was directed to the front pew with Colin, and he encouraged Georgia and Steve to sit by him as he was obviously in need of friendly faces around him.

The hearse arrived exactly on time, and the casket, with a tasteful arrangement of flowers on top, was reverently taken out and carried in by pallbearers in dark suits preceded by the vicar who had started into his ritual. The ceremony was a rather short one but included hymns that the vicar had suggested were ones that Stan might like because he had been heard to try and pick out the tunes as he was working.

Stan made no real attempt to join in with the singing, but during 'Morning Has Broken', he could be seen to be mouthing the words 'blackbird'. Enthusiastic singing of 'Jerusalem' by the congregation obviously stirred some distant memory, and a few tears ran down his cheek. Georgia remembered that it had always been a favourite when she was at the secondary school, and it must have been popular when Stan had been there some years before. She reflected on the inexplicable way that music can evoke emotions even if the memory of them is unclear. Something about that old school song had triggered a response, although he would have no recollection of when or where he had heard it. It was yet another thing hidden in the inaccessible recesses of his memory.

The vicar spoke a few words about Martha but thankfully did not attempt to deliver a full eulogy, which might have inferred that she would be sadly missed. He gave the outline of her life, briefly mentioning her daughter, Mary, and Stan without dwelling on the accident but stressing how much he was loved within the village and how much he had contributed to village life and the maintenance of the church and its surroundings. The vicar also made references to Stan's many animal friends in the churchyard who would be with him as he came to terms with his loss. Stan smiled briefly at this mention but otherwise seemed largely unmoved by the vicar's words.

After the short service, the vicar led the coffin and one or two of the mourners out to the prepared grave while the majority of the crowd headed off to the Trout or to get back to their places of work. Stan looked strangely uneasy by the grave. He had been around for a number of funerals, but he had always hung about discreetly in the background and yet here he was, centre stage. The vicar said a few appropriate words and then threw a few bits of soil into the grave. Stan looked confused but was encouraged to throw a bit of earth down onto his gran's casket. Georgia and Steve did likewise, followed by Colin and Mike Colly. Throughout this little ceremony, Stan's friends, the rooks, had perched silently up in one of the high trees as though even they wanted to treat the moment with the respect it deserved. This simple activity being completed, the majority of the little group headed off. Most went directly to the wake while Steve and Stan were left looking down at the coffin with its smattering of soil. Stan went over to one of the floral tributes that had been left and selected a single rose. He stood for a moment, looking down into the grave before offering his final farewell to the only relative he'd known for years.

"Sorry, Gran," he said as the tears flowed freely down his cheeks. "I love you, Gran, I'm sorry. Bye." With this, he gently let the flower fall from his hand onto the casket and then headed off to his shed to change. By the time Steve got back, Stan was well into his task, and the grave was filling up fast. Steve picked up the shovel that Stan had provided for him and started to help, but it was obvious that the procedure took particular skills, and Stan knew what he was doing. It was this expertise that had meant that the soil that had been removed had been placed on a large tarpaulin so when most of the earth had been shovelled into the grave, the two men were able to pull the tarpaulin over the grave to deposit a lot of the remainder. There was now a pronounced mound of earth over the grave, but Stan explained it would need to settle for a few months, and then he would get a nice headstone for her and one for his mum, as her grave had never had any commemorative adornment. Martha had obviously never felt the need to pay out for an elaborate headstone for her daughter's grave, which was marked only by a small stone with barely decipherable basic details of the occupant. The two men stood for a few moments; Stan was looking at the graves of the two people who had played a major part in his life, even though he could only remember one of them. After this short moment of reverence, Steve went off to change while Stan cleared up. The floral tributes were placed in the porch of the church to be used later to decorate the building, and then the tools were loaded onto his barrow and taken to the shed.

Having changed back into smarter clothes, Steve made a point of going up to the churchyard to make sure Stan hadn't changed his mind about going to the pub. Stan was sitting in his shed and had changed back into his suit but seemed to be waiting for instructions as to what he should do next. Since his recovery from his accident, Stan's life had been largely organised by his gran or governed by an inflexible regime, so all of the day's events were new to him, and he didn't know how to respond. Steve reassured him that there would be many friends in the pub who would love to see him, and the pair set off to the wake. When they arrived, Stan was met by a crowd of people, all wishing him well and giving their commiserations. He was clearly overawed by the attention. A number of the women hugged him, and it was quite obvious that this was a new sensation for the young man. At first, he appeared uncomfortable with this proximity to others but soon seemed to realise that he actually enjoyed it. His gran had never shown such overt affection towards him, and he had no recollection of his mother. He knew he'd had a girlfriend called Judy, but all he had was a photo of her and the fact that she had gone away; he had no memory of ever having been with her.

It was generally accepted as good fortune that Brad Carter had obviously decided not to try and crash the party, but the mystery of his whereabouts was a repeated subject in many of the conversations during the afternoon. Tony had arranged a substantial buffet, provided for in the late Mrs Turner's will and after a while, the atmosphere became more cordial as people discussed events in the village's recent history. It would be true to say that there were few anecdotes reflecting on any good qualities ever displayed by Martha. Most of the guests obeyed the advice not to speak ill of the dead, so little was mentioned of Stan's gran. Even he was soon seen to be enjoying himself as he set about attacking the buffet. He was obviously amazed at the fact that people kept offering him drinks and was quickly coming to terms with the fact that wakes could be good opportunities for social interaction despite his limited experience of socialising. He was even seen to laugh on a couple of occasions when Mark produced some of his jokes.

The wake was still going strong at nine in the evening, by which time the numbers had been swelled by people who had been unable to make the service due to work commitments. In the end, Colin suggested to Stan that it was getting late and it might be a good idea to leave. The truth was that Stan had enjoyed more beer than was usual for him, and it made good sense to get him home before he overdid it; Stan was not used to partying and meeting so many well-wishers on such an occasion. Before he left, he made it clear to Colin that he wanted to say something, so Monica was persuaded to ring the old 'last orders' bell.

The room fell silent as Monica announced that Stan wanted to have a few words. There was an awkward silence while Stan summed up the courage to make his announcement.

"I don't do the big speaking thing," he started. "My lovely gran has gone now, but I'll look after her and Mum. I want to say thank you to all my friends here for helping me say goodbye to Gran. She will be very happy. I miss her very much."

With that, Stan and Colin left with Mark, who blew his usual theatrical kisses to everyone.

"It's so annoying to see how much he doted on his gran despite the way she treated him over the years. He's like some big friendly dog who remains loyal to his mistress despite being regularly beaten," observed Steve. "He's the only one in the village who feels any tinge of remorse at her passing."

The wake went on for some time as people enjoyed the opportunity to meet up, and the dark shadow of Martha's memory was not allowed to spoil the fun. The absence of Brad Carter was a bonus as well, but the topic of his apparent disappearance punctuated a number of conversations during the evening, with everyone agreeing that his absence was a blessing.

The mystery of the missing drunk deepened the following day when a dog walker crossing the bridge happened to look down at the closest reed bed and saw what he took to be a half-empty bottle of whisky partially concealed in the tall stems. The dog walker, being aware of the last sighting of Carter by the bridge, thought it might be something to follow up. Resisting the temptation to try and retrieve the bottle himself, he informed the police and then stood around to see what would happen. The message apparently filtered down to PC Bright, who urgently headed to the bridge in detective mode. By the time he arrived, there was a small group of individuals peering over the parapet. The young police officer, eager to try and take control of the situation and to impress his audience, took a plastic bag from his pocket and set off to retrieve the bottle. Members of the crowd warned him about the unstable nature of the river bank at that spot, but he felt he knew better and pressed on with his quest. He managed to deftly pick up the bottle with the plastic bag so as not to mess up any evidence that might be on it. As he proudly displayed his prize to the spectators on the bridge, he neglected to heed their warnings about the questionable solidity of the bank and slid gracefully into the river. Fortunately, he was able to grab some of the strong reeds and avoided being dragged further into the water, but even so he was drenched almost up to his waist. Two men in the small crowd managed to get down and help him out of the fast-flowing water as he grasped the 'evidence' tenaciously.

As the soaking constable climbed up onto the bridge, one of the gathering pointed to a mark on the top of the parapet.

"What's that?" he asked. "It looks a bit like blood, and the dog seems interested in it."

Despite his bedraggled state, young Danny sprang into action.

"Don't touch it, please, sir, and can everyone stand clear of the spot? I'm declaring it a possible crime scene, so we'll have to get forensics on the case. Please move away from the spot; I'm going to have to call it in and get some assistance."

Danny was in his element. He was displaying his imagined authority over his civilian audience and playing out the dramatic role he had envisaged himself playing out for years. Needless to say, the local police emergency units did not break any speed records in responding to his call. In his short time in the service, he had gained a reputation for being quick to press the alarm button, and his general level of incompetence was recognised by all. Some of his previous exploits had gone down in local police lore. He had an indefatigable enthusiasm for reading all sorts of criminal malevolence into what turned out to be perfectly innocent events. His youthful enthusiasm was originally welcomed by his immediate superiors on the force, but they had tired of his tendency to over-dramatise everything. It had started when he found a child's bike in the middle of the road just outside the village. PC Bright had been reading about a recent child kidnapping case, and if he'd had his way, he would have called in several police cars, had the police helicopter called out and informed Interpol. As it turned out, a local recognised the bike, and the eight-year-old owner was located at his house nearby. Apparently, he had been trying some particular stunt, fallen off his bike and abandoned it to hobble home with a nasty grazed knee. It was generally acknowledged that bathing his knee and sticking on a plaster was a better response than alerting half the police services across Europe, as Danny might have suggested. It was his youthful enthusiasm that had led him to be called Vaulter at the station because of his tendency to jump to conclusions.

When two CID officers arrived, Danny was quick to update them on his theory as to what had happened, and they routinely listened to him before effectively ignoring him and inspecting the scene for themselves. Having obtained a brief history of what had been going on in the village from some of the small crowd that had gathered, the police officers declared that it was, indeed, a suitable case to call for specialists to examine the scene to try and establish what had happened. Danny was practically beaming with delight at the apparent recognition of his sleuthing but was less pleased when he was told to stand by and stop anyone interfering with the evidence while the specialist officers arrived. Thus it was that the young constable, soaked almost up to his waist, stood on scene guard and waited.

When the scene of crime officers arrived, Danny was eager to impart his specialist knowledge of the scene he had identified, but the team were keen to gather their own information and dutifully ignored most of what he had to say. This appeared to be the standard response from any of the local police officers who knew of Danny's previous exploits. Preliminary tests at the scene showed that it was indeed blood on the parapet, and samples were scraped off for further examination. Danny carefully handed over the whisky bottle in its plastic bag, and it was meticulously catalogued with all the other pieces of evidence. Numerous photographs were taken and measurements recorded before the specialists got into their van and drove off. Danny had asked if he might be able to get a lift home to quickly change his trousers, but the leader of the crime scene investigators said it might contaminate evidence. The truth was that she didn't want the smell of mud and river water in the van. While this was a disappointment to Danny as his house was at the far end of the village, he felt a sense of pride in being, how he perceived himself, a central figure in a murder investigation. In his mind, it had to be murder, and he never even considered the possibility of an accident or suicide. He had already started to draw up a mental list of potential murderers, and it was a rather long list.

CHAPTER EIGHT

For the next couple of days, the village was buzzing with the news of the events surrounding PC Bright's involvement in the incident on the bridge. It had soon become apparent that the whisky bottle had plenty of fingerprints, and all of them were from Brad Carter. The police had a record of his fingerprints and his DNA from his previous conviction. The fingerprints on the bottle were quickly matched with Carter's, but the DNA from the blood sample took a few days.

Danny Bright was eager to show his knowledge of the process and quickly concluded that there had obviously been some vicious assault on Carter by 'person or persons unknown' and his badly beaten body had been tipped into the river. There was no evidence to support this hypothesis, but that didn't bother Danny, and some of the locals were happy to accept this scenario if it meant that Carter would not return. In all fairness to Danny, it was not an unreasonable assumption, given the scanty evidence available at the scene.

The heavy rain of the previous week had largely passed through, and the river level had fallen, so the villagers were treated to the sight of police divers scouring the area downriver of the bridge. It was not an easy job as the river was still flowing quite quickly, and the mud that had been washed down made visibility a problem. The divers were limited to groping around in the murky water, feeling for what might be a body. While all this was going on, there were teams of police searching both banks of the river for some miles downstream. All of these measures failed to produce any evidence to prove whether or not Carter had been thrown, fallen or even jumped into the river. The DNA samples from the bridge parapet had proven to match those on police records from Carter. It was tentatively concluded that something had happened on the bridge and that Carter probably fell in the river and was swept away by the flood waters, but it was to be some time before any official announcement could be made. In the meantime, the police were examining Carter's caravan and his vehicle to see if they could offer up any clues as to his movements immediately before what may have happened on the bridge. Danny Bright was eager to tell everyone that he had made the initial search of the caravan and that the investigating officers had been impressed by his diligence. Nobody believed that Danny's contribution had been particularly valued, but in his world he was a central figure in the investigation. This period of uncertainty was the ideal breeding ground for rumours that circulated rapidly around the village.

Steve and Georgia were enjoying a quiet drink at the pub one evening when Tony informed them of the latest item of gossip to do the rounds in the village.

"Daft Danny has taken it upon himself to find as much as he can about the fate of Dan Carter," he announced as he pulled a pint for one of the other guests. "As you'd expect, the police are carrying out their formal investigations, hence their presence in the village as they talk to everyone, but Danny is determined to 'solve' the case himself. I've seen more of him in the Trout over the last couple of weeks than I would like to. He seems to think he's doing some special plain clothes duties in here, pumping the locals for information, as if nobody knows he's the local bobby living out some fantasy about being a valued police officer. He's not strong on subtlety as he uses all sorts of blatant ploys to turn any conversation to the events surrounding what he still refers to as the murder. He thinks he is cleverly leading his suspects into a false sense of security as he asks them about events on the day of the mysterious disappearance, but his intentions fool nobody."

"I'm sure we all have our suspicions about what might have happened," commented Georgia. "But there are so few definite facts. Carter's last reported sighting was by Mike Colly, who saw him on the bridge two days before the funeral, but after that, there's been nothing. So, if Carter went for a swim, it must have been sometime between then and the day after the funeral; that's quite a window of opportunity for something to have happened."

"And we mustn't lose sight of the fact that Carter might just stroll in here, completely unharmed," suggested Steve. "Heaven forbid! So who has Danny got in the frame so far?"

"Well, if you want to see it as current betting, then Mike Colly would appear to be the favourite. After his confrontation here with Carter, it is pretty obvious that they would never be exchanging Christmas cards. Mike's threat to forcibly eject the little weasel from the pub was witnessed by a lot of locals and the visiting White Horse cricket team. People still talk about the incident fondly, but despite the absence of any physical violence, it doesn't show Mike in a good light. Added to that, there's the fact that his mysterious army background and general fitness mean that he would have had no problem overpowering Carter and sending him downriver. Since the alleged incident, all the old rumours about Mike's supposed involvement in the special services have re-emerged, and of course, they have slowly become embellished. Now, the good old grapevine reports that he single-handedly destroyed an enemy arms depot during the Falklands War and was awarded a whole chest full of medals for it. Such a tough guy would have no problem seeing off Carter, and there is the fact that Mike is reputed to have been the last one to see Carter."

"If that's the word on the street," suggested Georgia, "then I'm surprised that Daft Danny hasn't arrested Mike by now."

"In the normal course of events," explained Tony, "if he had his way, he would have had Mike in for interrogation by now, but fortunately the police aren't nearly as quick to pick up the first person whose name crops up. Anyone who had the misfortune to have any meeting with Carter will appreciate that the list of the possible suspects doesn't stop with Mike. Bill was enraged when he saw what had been done to the cricket pitch, and there is little doubt that it was Carter in his pickup that did the damage. Bill is a relatively fit guy, and his prowess with the bat is well known around these parts. If he'd met Carter on the bridge, then a mighty blow would have knocked the rat straight over the parapet, with little need for the umpire to assess the strength of the stroke."

"There's always Colin to consider," suggested Steve. "He's one of the nicest guys you could wish to meet, but he was incensed at the way Carter spoke of Mark and his friends. Colin is naturally defensive of Mark, but even so, I don't think he'd be a front-runner; he's just too nice a guy."

"In terms of betting," continued Tony, "Colin is an outsider, but his odds are shorter than old Mrs Simpson. She was furious at the way Carter tried to kick little Snoopy. I somehow doubt that she would have had the strength to overpower Carter, though. On the other hand, with her pharmaceutical background, she might have slipped him a Mickey Finn and then helped him on his way over the parapet, but I don't think even Danny would come up with such a possibility. The fact is that all these incidents are common knowledge in the village, and it builds up a pretty damning picture of Carter which could have influenced any one of a large number of individuals to take it upon themselves to rid us of him. It wouldn't surprise me if Danny hasn't toyed with the idea of a group of vigilantes from the village plotting to sort Carter out, and I can think of several people who would, at the very least, have been prepared to 'look the other way' when the deed was done."

"I guess Stan must be a suspect in Danny's eyes," suggested Steve.

"Surely not Stan," protested Georgia. "He's such a gentle person."

"We know that," replied Steve. "But remember how Danny tried so hard to get Stan arrested for Martha's death. He refused to accept that it was an accident and seemed visibly disappointed and unconvinced when the postmortem findings were announced. I reckon that Danny would feel vindicated if he could get Stan for this 'murder'. There is also the fact that Stan had that bit of a confrontation with Carter in the pub, and there is also the slim chance that someone might have let it slip to Stan that Carter was the cause of the accident all those years ago on the bridge."

"Stan is so placid that even if he had known, it wouldn't have made him mad. He just accepts who he is now and has no perception of what life may have been like for him if he hadn't been involved in the crash, so he could have no thought of revenge," pointed out Georgia.

"There are dozens of potential subjects," added Tony. "You are a possible, for a start, Steve."

"Why me?"

"You've witnessed the confrontations in here involving Carter's brutish behaviour, and you are a member of the cricket team, so the vandalising of the pitch might be assumed to have annoyed you. On top of that, it's well known that you are a particular friend of Stan's. I know that nobody in their right mind would suspect you, but when it comes to Danny Bright, we are not talking about the greatest detective brain."

"You seem to have missed out one prime suspect, Tony," added Georgia cheekily. "You. You've been present much of the time when the incidents in the pub occurred, and you are the one that barred him. On top of that, you were furious when Carter allegedly broke the window, and you stayed up all night, threatening to catch him if he came again."

"I can't pretend that I didn't have a motive, like so many others in the village, and there is also the fact that, as far as I know, I don't have an alibi because we don't know exactly when the alleged incident took place."

"Agatha Christie would sort it out by gathering all the suspects in a room," added Steve. "And then the famous detective would eliminate them one by one before exposing the killer. The problem is that, in our case, the detective would be Daft Danny Bright, renowned for his ineptitude. The other complication is that it would be hard to find a room big enough to accommodate all the suspects."

"I can't think of anybody in the village who would claim to be saddened by Carter's departure," commented Steve. "But his disappearance has left a feeling of unfinished business. There's been no sense of 'closure', as they say. After all that initial mystery over Martha's death and Danny's reluctance to see it as natural causes, it wouldn't surprise me if he still harbours some thought that we might have a serial killer in the village."

"Thanks for floating that idea," added Georgia. "It's a good job we don't all share Danny's habit of trying to over-dramatise everything, or we wouldn't be able to sleep soundly in our beds at night."

"It's a good job you've got me to protect you at night," suggested Steve.

"Assuming you're not the serial killer," added Georgia jokingly. "But I think I'll risk it and allow you to take me home."

Life in the village settled back into something more like normality as the mystery of Carter's disappearance became less of a subject of conversation, but memories of him re-emerged after a short report on the local TV news. Steve had returned home one Friday after a heavy day in the factory, and he slumped down in front of the television with Georgia, as was their habit. They were always particularly interested to see what the weather forecast was for the region for the weekend, but their attention was drawn to a report on the discovery of a body in the river downstream of Hartbridge. The couple sat in silence to catch what the young TV reporter was saying as a recording of her on the river bank was played.

"Reports have been confirmed about a body that has been found on what is locally called Otter Island near Newport. Emergency services were called to the area yesterday afternoon when a fisherman in his boat moored up to the island and caught sight of a body in the reeds. Police have stated that no official identification has yet been made, but it is said to be a man who was reported missing recently, and his family have been informed. The police have stated that this incident should act as a reminder to the public that the river can be dangerous, especially after the recent heavy rain."

"Otter Island is nearly nine miles downstream," observed Georgia. "It just goes to show the strength of the current to move Carter so far."

"It certainly confirms our suspicions that the river must have been in full flood when he fell into the water. Or was he pushed?"

"Don't start that; you're starting to sound like Daft Danny. One conspiracy theorist is more than enough in one village."

After dinner, the couple decided to wander down to the pub to celebrate the start of the weekend and to catch up on the latest gossip about the late Dan Carter.

"It's good news as far as I'm concerned," commented Tony as he poured out drinks for Georgia and Steve. "It's good to have that shadow of doubt removed and to know that the offensive creep won't be coming back. Good riddance to him; I've yet to meet anyone who isn't glad to see he's gone. I'm tempted to have a party to celebrate the fact that he's turned up dead, but I guess that might be deemed to be in bad taste."

"What about his family?" asked Georgia. "The news report said that the family had been informed, but I didn't know he had any family. Mrs Holland at the post office said that she heard he had inherited from his mother when she died, and I never heard any mention of his father or any other family members."

"I didn't know he had relatives; I thought his sort were spawned, not born," added Tony with ill-concealed contempt.

"Be careful what you say about him," warned Steve playfully, "or you'll go straight to the top of Danny's list of murder suspects. I bet he's eagerly awaiting the outcome of the coroner's report. It wouldn't surprise me if our local sleuth hadn't set up his bedroom as an incident room with pictures of all the suspects pinned to his wall."

"He'd need a bloody big wall," commented Tony as he turned to serve some other customers.

As the evening progressed, the discovery of the body was a central point of discussion. There were the usual questions about the sequence of events that could have caused Carter to enter the water and a general interest in the strength of the current needed to carry a body so far. It was agreed that if the body had not been caught up in one of the many reed beds, then it could eventually have been swept out to sea to be picked over by the crabs, and no one would have had any idea what happened to it. At least there was confirmation of Carter's death, even if the cause was still uncertain.

The sense of satisfaction in the village at the news that Carter had been found turned out to be somewhat premature. The following morning was planned as a leisurely start as Steve was not working that Saturday. After breakfast, Georgia was about to go down and open the shop while Steve switched on the television to catch the news. After watching for a while, he was about to switch off the set when he picked up a mention of a recently discovered body in the river. He stopped, with his finger about to depress the power button on the remote, and listened attentively as the local presenter made an announcement.

"It has been announced that the body retrieved from Otter Island recently is that of Nigel Marker. The 68-year-old had left the Lasker House retirement home on what had been one of his regular walks along the river bank to visit the Duke of York public house in Newport. On his failure to return, staff at the home alerted police, but initial searches failed to find Mr Marker. It is suspected that he may have slipped into the river and drowned. The coroner has been informed."

Steve immediately went down to the shop to update Georgia on the latest news.

"It's just been on the local news," he blurted out. "The body that turned up on Otter Island wasn't Carter. It seems that it was a guy from a local retirement home who they think might have slipped into the river. It's not clear what happened, but it was definitely not Carter."

"Oh Hell! Just when we thought we could draw a veil over the whole issue of Carter, we find it's far from settled."

"It does highlight how dangerous the river can be, and it's still likely that Carter came to a similar end and could be feeding the fishes out at sea by now. If the river could carry one poor soul for some distance, then is it too much to hope that it did the same for Carter?"

"Yes, everything seemed cleared up. Now we know nothing. There's no body, and we are in a state of limbo. Carter's car is still parked down by the caravan he owns. He could turn up today, having been on one of the lengthiest benders in history, and just get on with his offensive life."

"I was talking with Don at work, and his father had told him that a missing person couldn't usually be declared dead for seven years even when it seems pretty obvious what had happened. It's a depressing prospect, but I have a feeling that we won't be seeing Carter again. Or is that just wishful thinking?"

"The police don't seem to have any leads to follow; the forensic work is ongoing, but all it seems likely to prove is that something dramatic happened on the bridge. At least we can be relieved to see that the 'real' police are on the case and not just Daft Danny Bright. The more I think of it, the more I feel that Danny's parents were the perpetrators of a cruel, ironic joke when they endowed their child with such a singularly inappropriate surname."

"There is one other consideration with the discovery of poor old Mr Marker on Otter Island," mused Steve. "In that it introduces a possible third mystery death for Danny to weave into his assessment of what happened. He'll be in his element, conjuring up all sorts of possibilities."

"And he will be looking for patterns to establish where the serial killer will strike next," added Georgia as she carried out her own mental audit of the situation before declaring, "The victims were Turner, Carter and Marker; they all rhyme!"

"Spooky!" he added. "If Danny notices that, then he will be asking for round-the-clock police protection for everyone in the village with a surname ending in *er*. We really shouldn't joke about it, but Danny brings it on himself. The one redeeming feature is that the regular police officers are fully aware of Danny's incompetence, so they are not going to jump into action every time he has a suspicion that something needs urgent investigation."

CHAPTER NINE

As the weeks passed and the long summer days gave way to the early autumn, life in the village went on at its steady pace. The earth over Martha's grave had settled a bit, and Stan inspected it regularly to monitor when it would be appropriate to have the memorial stone placed on it. With some help from Colin, he had ordered two headstones to be made up. He planned to install the one for his mother at the same time that he set up his gran's. He was often joined in the churchyard by Mike, and they would chat for hours as they sat on one of the benches or when the older man was helping Stan with some of the routine work around the church. The two had set up a real friendship, the worldly ex-soldier and the innocent young lad whose experiences were limited to the years he had spent in the village since his accident.

It was a somewhat unusual relationship. They could sit for long periods of time with neither of them saying anything, but the silences were not uncomfortable. Their conversations were largely limited to their observations on their joint interest in the natural history of the churchyard; Stan would introduce his friends to Mike, and the older man would impart his own knowledge of the local flora and fauna. They spent a long time sitting in silence, and eventually many of the creatures that had come to trust Stan became less wary of Mike. They rarely discussed the past; Mike was always reticent about his army days, and Stan knew precious little about his own past. He would occasionally mention his former girlfriend, Judy, when reminded of the name by his special robin turning up.

One subject that they never discussed was the mysterious Dan Carter, whose fate was something that both men preferred to forget. They did have limited conversations about events in the village, but Stan was unaware of the social undercurrents around him, and Mike was largely uninterested in any form of gossip.

This odd couple were sometimes joined by Steve, who enjoyed spending a few quiet moments in the churchyard. He would often wander over from the florists if Georgia was busy in the shop. Late one Saturday morning, he arrived with news for his friends.

"Hi Mike, Stan," he greeted them, "I've got a job. I've just had a letter from the water company, and they've offered me a post."

"Congratulations, lad," said Mike. "You must feel a lot more secure about your future now; the job at the factory was handy, but it was only a seasonal contract."

"Yes, but it's strange that I will have a starting salary at the water board that will be considerably less than the pea factory paid out. But, as Georgia so rightly points out, I should be better off in the long run. She's delighted by the fact that at least one of us has a possible career to look forward to. She's still applying for jobs, but as I know to my cost, a degree is no longer a guarantee of quickly finding a good career. Fortunately, she can continue working in the shop, which brings in some money and puts a roof over our heads."

"I did a degree," added Stan, as he remembered something his gran had said to him on many occasions, but he had no idea just what a degree was, and its value to him had been lost, with so much more, after his accident.

"I was never the scholarly type," declared Mike. "I did reasonably well at school, but I wanted to get away from home as soon as I could, and I couldn't stand the thought of staying on for an extra two years. It wasn't a bad home life, but we were never a close family, and on top of that, I felt that I needed to 'spread my wings'. I felt that my mother was always getting at me, complaining that I was treating the house like a hotel and not taking responsibility for any chores around the place. As I look back, I realise that she was right. I contributed very little to the running of the house and generally just created more work for her. I'm afraid I was like a younger version of my dad, but at least he brought money into the home even if he did no work when he was there."

Steve recognised that this was a rare insight into Mike's past, and he took the opportunity to find out more about his new friend.

"So what did you decide to do?" he asked tentatively.

"The options were rather limited. I was pretty good at sports and eager to learn some sort of trade, so I applied for the army. Quite frankly, there were very few career options up in the North East at that time for people who left school with few formal qualifications, and the army offered me accommodation, so I signed up as soon as I could. It wasn't a bad life as a young man, and I was set on becoming an electrical engineer."

"So, did that work out for you?"

"Not exactly. It was great fun for a while, a bit of travel, a range of sports, some girls, and mates you could share a few jars with on some pretty wild nights out. Much the same as university life is made out to be, but without the fees," he said with a wry smile. "It was an interesting time in my life but hardly what you would describe as a settled existence."

"And did you manage to get the training that you wanted? My dad always said that you couldn't go wrong if you had a trade; he tried to persuade me to become a joiner because it was a 'real job' in his eyes."

"I did get stuck in and applied myself. It seemed that the army suited me, or perhaps I suited the army, and I was doing very well with the prospect of a bit of promotion. I regarded it as a career and, like many of the chaps, I had mapped out my future, even to the point when I would be able to retire and what rank I would have achieved, but it was not to be. It all changed with the Iranian Embassy siege in 1980. It was covered extensively on the TV when the SAS blew their way in to rescue the hostages."

"I've seen old clips on the telly and watched a documentary on the siege. It was like something out of an action movie," commented Steve.

"It was all so dramatic, and many of us young lads in the army dreamed of becoming like those heroes abseiling into the embassy. There was a mystique about the Special Forces and an undeniable respect for them. Like so many young men, I arrogantly thought that I would apply to join, they would see how fit I was, and I would fly through the entrance tests. I soon saw that I was not to be seen as God's gift to the SAS; the training was nothing short of brutal, but I eventually got in. From then on, I was part of a strange shadowy force who were often sent in to do jobs that the general public could know nothing about. We had to be ready to go anywhere we were needed in the world at a moment's notice. We had to be constantly in a state of readiness, and that in itself put a great strain on us. The secrecy of some of our missions meant that we couldn't share our experiences with loved ones, so we had to get through it all with just the support of our mates in the service. It was far harder than many had anticipated. In some ways, being on an operation was the easier part. It was often physically demanding and dangerous, but at least we were doing the job we were designed for, and we got a great feeling of satisfaction when we did that job well."

"I've got to admit that I would not have been able to cope with that lifestyle," added Steve. "It all sounds very exciting, but I prefer my quiet life with Georgia."

"Just before I went into the Special Service, I had met a girl called Mary, and my change in career direction was disastrous for that relationship. I had been briefly transferred to Callerthorpe Camp for some reason best known to the army, and I met Mary at a dance there."

The older man paused for a moment as if remembering some happier time in his life before resuming his story.

"We were quite an item, and our relationship quickly developed. It still seems strange to me that there I was, the archetypal young squaddie, supposedly searching out sex at every opportunity, but it was Mary who obviously wanted to progress our relationship. I foolishly thought that she was keen to get married, and it was apparent from what she said that she was as eager to get away from home as I had been. Obviously, I had misread the signs, and she suddenly went off me. The whole situation was a mess that was made worse by the Falklands War. It was the very nature of the unit that we had to be available at 24 hours' notice to fly out anywhere in the world. No time for the niceties of sorting out your social calendar: the army said you had to move and when you had to move. I had no time to discuss the whole thing with Mary. I was afraid she might think I was just walking out on her, so as soon as operational protocol allowed, I wrote to explain, but I received no response. I tried writing quite a few times when I was able to do so.

"Immediately after the Falklands issue, my unit was deployed to Northern Ireland, so it was many months before I could manage to briefly get back to the village. I knew her address by heart, *Malvinas Cottage*. It was in the High Street, here in Hartbridge. As the Argentinian government claimed the Falklands under their name as The Malvinas, it was a hard name to forget. I wasn't sure how Mary would respond to my presence after she'd left me, so I only had a brief look around the village one afternoon, but there was no such cottage, and I assumed the whole thing had been a cruel deception, so I left. I thought things had been so good between us, but I had obviously been fooling myself."

"Did you stay in the unit for long?" asked Steve, surprised at Mike's sudden openness about his past.

"No. It all sounded so attractive to me as a young man, with all the implied excitement and adventure, but the truth is that it's very demanding, both physically and emotionally. I didn't mind the need to keep in peak physical shape and actually relished the challenges of some of the training exercises we had to go through. The operational pressure could be quite difficult; it often involved a degree of danger and some of the things we were called upon to do put an immense strain on us. Sustaining a family life or a relationship of any sort was extremely difficult, so, in a way, it shouldn't have surprised me that my relationship with Mary failed. I transferred to another regiment after a few years, both for my own mental health and for better promotional prospects. I did relatively well, and after some years in Yorkshire, I ended up back at Callerthorpe in a cushy little training job. I still harboured some pathetic hope of meeting up with Mary again, but I guess by then she would have been settled down with children. I searched the village more thoroughly, but it seems that the name and address that she had given me were false. She played me like a fool, and like a fool, I was eager to accept more of the same."

"She was a silly woman to leave you," proffered Stan. "My friend Judy was at the camp, but she had to go away." He had only understood part of Mike's story, but he obviously felt some empathy for his friend who, like him, had lost his girlfriend.

As the three men sat and enjoyed feeding the birds and exchanging inconsequential discussions, the first heavy drops of rain began to fall. This was not the sort of rain that demanded a quizzical look to the heavens to see if it actually was raining. This rain made its presence known in sudden heavy drops that quickly turned into a deluge, and the three men automatically ran to Stan's shed to escape a certain soaking. Stan instinctively filled the kettle and put it on the stove while suggesting that his guests should take a seat. This posed a problem because Stan only had functional seating for two, but he made it clear that he would sit on what appeared to be a large wooden tool chest. Thus, the three of them sat and waited for the kettle to boil. For a while, they listened to the rain beating down on the shed roof, and there was a general sense of light-heartedness like three schoolboys enjoying a soggy camping expedition.

"I guess that's Judy there," declared Mike, as he looked over at the blurred black-and-white photograph that hung on the shed wall. The young woman in the picture was somewhat indistinct, possibly because she had moved slightly as the picture was being taken, but she was standing by a staircase that Mike recognised immediately as the one in the reception hall of the camp at Callerthorpe.

"No, that's not Judy," declared Stan, with a little laugh. "That's Mum."

He wandered over and looked at the picture, and his mood became slightly melancholic as he gazed at the indistinct image.

"Gran wouldn't let me have it at home, so I brought it here. I don't remember Mum. Gran didn't talk about her, but

I wanted my picture. Gran didn't like Mum, and we didn't have many pictures of her, but I found this one. This is my picture."

Mike said nothing and sat in pensive silence as Stan busied himself making the cups of tea and offering chocolate biscuits to his guests. The biscuits were a little luxury that he allowed himself now that he had access to more of his own money. While Stan and Steve exchanged views on the desirability of having a good rain shower to benefit the gardens, Mike continued to sit in silence before sharing his thoughts.

"What was your mum's name, Stan?"

"Mum."

"What was her other name?"

"Mary. Gran always called her 'your mother'. She didn't talk about her much, but I don't think she liked her. She never said anything nice about her. I don't think she was a good mum, but she was my mum."

"How old are you now, Stan?" Mike persisted with his questioning.

"I don't know. I'm not good at numbers. Gran always did the numbers. It might be in my diary."

"You keep a diary?" asked Steve with a degree of surprise in his voice.

"It's good to keep a diary, to write things in that you do. It was on the TV."

"And is the diary at home?" asked Mike with a mounting sense of interest.

"No. Gran wouldn't like that."

"So you don't actually keep a diary?"

"Yes, it's good to keep a diary. They said so on *Blue Peter*."

"So where is it?" asked Mike, trying hard not to be seen to be pressurising Stan with what was in danger of becoming a barrage of questions.

"In my collection. Gran wouldn't let me keep some things in the house, so I keep them here. Over in my box. It's my special collection."

He stood up from the wooden chest and carefully opened the heavy lid. At first glance, the box appeared to be empty, but Stan leant over and took a battered old box file from the recesses of his former seat. He opened it reverently and took out a small diary, which he gave to Mike, who looked at the cover, smiled and said, "This diary is for 1993."

"Yes, it's good to keep a diary. They said so on *Blue Peter*."

"Well, you've certainly kept that one for a long time," conceded Mike, passing the diary for Steve to look at. As he idly glanced through the book, which, like most diaries, was largely empty, he happened upon an early page with the basic information, "*This diary belongs to Stanley Turner, aged eleven.*"

"So that means that you were born in about 1982, assuming you put the inscription in when you first got the diary."

Stan was not largely impressed with this piece of information, but he nodded politely. His thoughts were taken up by some of the other items in his precious collection, and Steve caught a glimpse of some of the treasures that Stan methodically took out and glanced at before putting them back. Stan seemed particularly occupied with a small trophy with a footballer figure on the top and a few medals that had presumably been awarded to the young Stan at some time in his school career. There was a cardboard roll that Steve recognised as the sort used to keep certificates recording academic achievements. Stan looked at some of the articles before returning them to his secret place. He had a collection of mementoes that he knew were important, but they evoked no memories for him; they were icons from someone else's life. Steve took the diary again and methodically went through the pages until he found what he had hoped would be there.

"Here it is," he announced triumphantly. "A starred entry on the seventeenth of December with the clear information, '*My birthday today, aged 11, went to have a party with mum and gran. Got red jumper from mum.*' That clears it up, Stan. You were born on December the seventeenth, 1982."

Once again, Stan seemed to find the fact to be of little relevance to him, but Mike was eagerly soaking up this information. The trio sat in the shed and waited for the worst of the rain to pass. Steve wanted to get back to the shop for lunch, but there was little point in getting soaked in the process. Periodically, he would look out of the open shed doorway to assess whether the rain was easing, and after a quarter of an hour, he felt slightly optimistic about the conditions and declared his intention to make a dash for home. Mike announced that he ought to be getting home as well, so the two men stood in the open doorway like parachutists waiting for the right moment to leap from the security of their plane. The rain had indeed eased somewhat, so they left the sanctuary of the shed and set off down the church path towards the road, but the rain had not finished with them, and by the time they reached the lychgate, it was coming down in torrential sheets again, and the men were glad to reach the relative shelter of the old oak structure.

"I think our dash for freedom might have been a bit premature," suggested Steve as he stood and looked across the road at the welcoming sight of the florist shop. "I don't think we can stay here all day, Mike. Why don't we make a quick run for the shop?"

"It seems odd that twenty-odd years ago, a bit of a shower like this would have seemed like nothing to me, and a structure such as this lychgate would have been like luxury accommodation," said Mike, with a smile. "But, right now, your plan is a very attractive one."

After dramatically, and quite unnecessarily, counting down from three, the two men launched themselves into the rain again and soon arrived at the shop, where Georgia was surprised to see the state they were in. She quickly ushered them upstairs and provided towels for them to dry off the worst excesses of water.

"You look like a pair of drowned rats," she announced. "I'll make you a hot drink while the pair of you stand in front of the gas fire and try and dry out a bit."

After a short time, the two men were looking more human, and Georgia joined them for a cup of tea. Rita was manning the shop, although the continuing rain meant that there was little likelihood of many customers popping in.

"This lot seems to have sprung up from nowhere," said Georgia, gesturing to the rain that was pelting down on the window. "It was fine earlier, and I'd even started to put a few buckets of flowers outside the shop, but that plan had to be aborted. How was Stan this morning?"

"Stan was just Stan," answered Steve. "He's like an island of calm; whatever is going on never ruffles him. As long as he has his friends, he is perfectly content with his lot. In a way, it's a blessing that he doesn't appreciate how his life might have been but for the accident. Ignorance may not always be bliss, but it can protect you from some pretty nasty parts of reality. We did learn a couple of things about him this morning, though, and even found out his date of birth."

"I'm surprised that he remembered that."

"He had no idea and wasn't at all interested, but he had an old 1993 diary which happened to show his eleventh birthday. Oh, and we also discovered that the old picture he has on the wall of his shed isn't his girlfriend Judy but his mum. Apparently, his gran didn't like pictures of her daughter around the house. It's almost as if she wanted to just erase her from history.

Poor Stan doesn't have any pictures of Judy at all, and he keeps waiting for someone he has absolutely no memory of."

"The old crone wanted to rewrite the family history to suit her own version of it," added Georgia. "She was furious when Mary wanted to retain her father's name when he died."

"Mary?" asked Mike eagerly. "So what was her surname?"

"Martha wanted her to adopt the surname Turner, but Mary always insisted on referring to herself as Mary Truelove. I think it was her one way of showing her rebellious side. Stan wasn't so bothered about his name, and he was amenable to his gran's request that he should change his surname to Turner, and he was always known as that from then on. It was just one more example of how she wanted to control him."

"So that picture in the shed is of Mary Truelove, not Mary Turner?" said Mike, as certain of his suspicions were being supported by further revelations about Mary. He sat in silence for a few minutes as he slowly processed all the new information he was getting.

"And Mary lived here in Hartbridge?" The latter statement was not so much a question but more of an attempt to confirm a fact that he was becoming increasingly aware of. "But she didn't live at Malvinas Cottage; I know because I searched the High Street for it. Was there some other property in the village with a similar name, Malvinas House, or just Malvinas? I wrote to Mary at Malvinas Cottage many times but never had a reply."

"After the Falklands conflict, I imagine that the name Malvinas wasn't popular in this country, so it's likely that the owners changed the name about that time," suggested Georgia. "I don't know a lot about it as I was born after the Falklands War. In fact, I know very little about the conflict except that it involved Argentinian forces taking over the island and South Georgia. It would be hard for me to forget that name because

Mum tells me that I was given my name, Georgia, because she liked the sound of it. I guess that I should be grateful that I didn't get called South Georgia."

"I wrote to my girlfriend, so why didn't I get any reply?" asked Mike, but the question was directed at himself as much as towards the others. "I wrote frequently to a Mary Truelove in Malvinas cottage but never got a reply. Why didn't she reply? I thought we were engaged in all but name, but I must have been mistaken. That bloody war screwed everything up. We were getting along so well, but then the army packed me off to the South Atlantic. I wish I'd had time to talk to her face-to-face, and I could have explained that I wasn't just deserting her. I tried to explain it in a lengthy letter but didn't even get a response. I couldn't phone her as she was always reluctant to give me her number. I think she was afraid that I might ring her, and her mother could have answered the phone and found out about our budding romance. I tried writing many times over the next few months, whenever my complicated military duties enabled me to put pen to paper, but not even an acknowledgement. And all that time she was still living here in the village. I just don't understand it; I just can't believe it."

"I think you might have hinted at a reason for the lack of replies to your letters," suggested Georgia. "Martha was an extremely controlling woman. You've seen how she was so protective of Stan, to the point of being domineering; well, she was the same with Mary. I think that there's a strong possibility that she opened your letters to her daughter and chose to destroy them rather than let her see them. She all but hid Mary away when it was discovered that she was pregnant, and the poor woman never escaped her clutches."

Mike's mind had been reeling with the emergence of the fact that Mary had probably not simply walked out of his life, but there was another inescapable question that was emerging;

could it be that the son his Mary had brought up was his? He carried out some quick calculations. They had established from Stan's old diary that he was born on the 17th of December 1982. Mike had abruptly been called away to the Falklands in early April of that year. Mike's brain raced through some elementary calculations. Could it be true? He went through the calculations again, counting out the months on his fingers. He was no expert but calculated that Mary must have only recently become pregnant at the time he was called away. He knew Mary would not have had any other partners at the time, so the young man he had spent so much time with, over the last few weeks in particular was, in his own mind, undoubtedly his son.

Georgia had watched Mike carefully and was aware of his mental turmoil. She had come up with the possibility of Stan being Mike's son before he had. It was as if the whole issue was something that the ex-soldier didn't dare to think possible. All the disclosures of the day had hit him in a way that his training could never have prepared him for. He was now faced with the twin possibilities that the love of his life had not walked out on him, and he may have a son he never knew about. Georgia had watched as Mike had surreptitiously counted out the months on his fingers. The pair looked at each other in silence; there was an understanding that didn't need to be discussed. A few moments later, Steve became aware of a strange silence, and then the possibility of Stan's parentage eventually dawned on him.

CHAPTER TEN

Mike sat in the flat above the florists with his two young friends. "Well, that's something I wasn't expecting," he commented unnecessarily. "For all these years, I thought I'd done something to upset Mary. I imagined that my sudden disappearance had led her to think I'd abandoned her, and now I realise that she was pregnant when I left. The poor love must have felt that I didn't care. I was called back to base in early April when the Falklands issue blew up, and I never saw Mary again. She must have been in the very early stages of her pregnancy because Stan was born in late December, and that bitch of a mother didn't tell Mary that I was trying desperately to contact her. Why did she do that? Things could have been so different."

"From what you've said, it seems that Stan is your son," commented Steve. "But I think it would be as well to prove it before you announce it, particularly to Stan."

"Of course he's my son. Mary wouldn't have gone out with anyone else when she was seeing me," said Mike with a slight hint of irritation in his voice.

"We can tell from your account that it's pretty certain that you are the father," interjected Georgia. "But before you wander up to Stan and announce that he's your son, you ought to be absolutely sure. What if Stan was a premature baby conceived after your departure? I don't see it being even remotely likely, but claiming parentage is a major issue. You have to be sure. Just because you want something to be true is no guarantee that you're right."

"That's what I was trying to get at," said Steve. "Everything you've said about Mary supports the notion that Stan is your son. Even looking at the pair of you. It is clear that you have certain similarities in that you are both tall and well-built, and you share certain facial features and even green eyes, but that, in itself, is not proof of anything."

"It's bloody annoying to think that I've spent years blaming the Falklands War for the breakdown of my relationship with Mary. It didn't help, and being moved all over the place with the regiment over the next couple of years was never conducive to a stable relationship, but now I realise that the main cause of my problem was Mary's mother. She appears to have just sat at home like some malevolent spider with her web restricting the activities of Mary and then Stan."

"Did you never get married or settle down with anyone, Mike?" asked Georgia in an attempt to move the conversation away from the obnoxious Mrs Turner.

"I've made a few attempts to get some stability in my life with some women, and even talked about getting married at one time, but it never worked out. I know it sounds daft, but I took a long time to get over Mary. For some years, I held on to the futile hope that we would get back together, and for a while I judged all new girlfriends by her standard. We had been just so perfect together, and I wanted every relationship to hit those heights from the start, which was grossly unfair on the women I met. Being in the SAS didn't help to sustain a relationship; it takes a special kind of woman to have a husband or partner who can be called away at a few hours' notice. That was part of the reason why I opted out after a few years. I didn't mind the intensive physical training and got a kick out of the excitement the work offered, but there is a finite limit to how long you can put up with that hectic lifestyle. After that, I moved through a number of posts and then just got my head down and waited for my retirement. My last post in Callerthorpe completed the circle of my career, but there was no Mary there anymore."

The group sat in silence for a while before Georgia began to formulate what should be their response to the day's findings.

"I know it must be tempting for you to inform people of your deductions, Mike," she surmised. "But I really think we ought to keep this to ourselves until we can devise a plan to establish the facts surrounding Stan's parentage. If certain people hear about this, then it will be spread throughout the village and taken as gospel. We must make sure that we keep it our secret for now."

"I know you're right," conceded Mike, "but I just want to put things right. I want Stan to know that he wasn't deserted. It's the only thing I can do. The greatest sadness for me is that Mary thought I'd walked out on her; I broke her heart and knew nothing about it, just as she broke mine, but it wasn't her fault. It's a good job her mother isn't still around because I'd have difficulty controlling my anger after what she did. It's so frustrating to think how things might have taken a different course if I hadn't been posted out to the Falklands and if Mary had received my letters. I was trained to cope with difficult situations. I had to get through times when I was put under almost impossible conditions, and I came through it, but looking back at the way things fell apart with Mary fills me with a feeling of being powerless. No amount of training could have prepared me to face up to the loss of Mary, and it's now too late. I know that it's futile to dwell on things you can't change, but I can't help but think how close we came to being happy together, and it's just so unfair."

He sat in silence for a while and covertly wiped a tear from his eye. Georgia was struck by the fact that this impressive figure of a man who'd had to face up to all manner of physical deprivation in often life-threatening situations had been made to feel impotent when he had to come to terms with the loss of the one love in his life. After a short while, Mike straightened up as if to reassert himself after what he had regarded as a minor loss of dignity and reaffirmed his intention to do what he could do, albeit at this late stage, to help Stan.

"I know it's not supported by anything, but I've recently come to feel some affinity with Stan, and we both enjoy our chats together. It's possibly just with the benefit of hindsight, but I feel there is something special there. I *know* he is my son, and I'll do everything I can to help him."

The worst of the rain seemed to have passed through, and Mike, having thanked Georgia and Steve for their hospitality, set off home.

"That was rather unexpected," commented Georgia after their guest had left. "I've never known Mike discuss his past before. With him being in the Special Forces, I thought that he would never discuss his army days; something to do with the Official Secrets Act or some such."

"When I think about it," observed Steve, "he never actually discussed his army life in any detail, but I think he wanted a chance to share his feelings and latterly his doubts. I guess that he wouldn't want to discuss such things in the surroundings of a pub. The bar is a good place to meet up and share experiences with friends, but sometimes you want an environment that is a little more intimate. The relative privacy of a gardener's shed is somehow strangely more conducive to sharing feelings if you feel comfortable with those around you. I must admit that suddenly getting so much information from him was a bit of a surprise."

"If all we've discussed proves to be right, then it will kill off a lot of the rumours in the village about Stan's parentage," commented Georgia. "As I've said before, just about every male in the vicinity of an appropriate age has been suggested as Stan's dad. Even my own father was in the frame, according to some gossip-mongers. That would have made Stan my half-brother, and as a young girl, I did wonder about having him as my older brother. I never believed it to be likely, but, like many only children, the possibility of an older brother was an attractive proposition, particularly one who had achieved such notable success as Stan had as a young man."

"Didn't you say Mike had once been a contender for having been Stan's father?"

"Yes, but I think it was only because he was perceived as the mysterious stranger with a background in some secretive army career. If it is ever proved that Mike is Stan's dad, then a lot of people will no doubt claim to have known it all along."

"We'll just have to see how things pan out," suggested Steve. "But in the meantime, we need to discuss the job I've been offered at the water company. It all looks very promising, but we need to make sure that it's what we both want."

"You've got to take it, and we'll fit our lives around it. One of us needs to get a job pretty soon. It's great to have the florist job as it literally gives us a roof over our heads, but we need to look towards a more settled future."

"Assuming that I take up the post, it's clear that I would probably have to move to Huntingdon at some point, but the information from the company implies that I would be working in this general area for a while so we could stay here until you find a post that might mean us moving. The water company cover a large area, and there are probably a number of places that I could spend time. It all depends on the exact nature of the particular scheme I'm attached to."

"And what sort of things will you be doing?"

"I don't know exactly, but it's all linked with the company's policy on biodiversity and environmental safeguards being established. Current politics and public opinion are pushing such issues to the fore. My post could be anything to do with factors affecting water quality in any of the local rivers, lakes or wetlands. I could find I spend time working with other agencies on the marshes just over the river near here. Whatever project I'm on, I'll probably spend my first few weeks observing and making the tea."

"I think the job will suit you. I had worried that you would be sitting in a water treatment plant in a white coat, monitoring water quality in test tubes."

"Heaven forbid! But right now, in preparation for my new post, why don't I take some of our delicious local water and make us another cup of tea?"

"Good idea, and I will make us a quick sandwich for lunch before I get back to work."

After lunch, Steve joined Georgia and Rita in the shop. While he claimed that he was there to help, his main reason for wanting to be there was to continue discussing his job offer and to share his hopes for the future with Georgia. As they discussed their plans for the life that was opening up before them, with all its promise, he couldn't help but think of the way fate had dealt with Mike and Stan so cruelly, and he resolved never to take his good fortune for granted. It was while he was in this positive state of mind that he announced his immediate plan.

"It's not every day that one is offered what appears to be a very promising career opportunity," he announced. "So I suggest that we go out to the Trout for dinner tonight when you've finished here."

"I suppose we ought to wait at least until the job pays you something, but I think we deserve a small celebration."

"Why don't you finish a bit earlier?" Rita offered. "And then you can get to the pub before the evening rush. The place often gets a bit full of people wanting to eat on a Saturday evening, but that's usually later on."

"That's very kind of you, Rita," said Steve. "But please don't tell Daisy that her daughter bunked off early; you know what a slave-driver she is."

"I don't think Mum will create too much fuss, and anyway, I'll just say you forced me; you know she would forgive you anything."

When the young couple arrived at the Trout to celebrate Steve's offer of employment, it was relatively empty. Colin was standing by the bar while Mark and his girlfriend Celia were sitting together on one of the bench seats. They were obviously deep in conversation because Mark didn't rush over to serenade Georgia or to tell one of his jokes. Steve ordered drinks, and then, noticing Colin's quiet disposition, he politely asked how things were going with his friend.

"It's Mark's birthday soon, and it's posing a few problems," said Colin quietly so that Mark couldn't hear what was being said.

"Why don't you join Georgia and me?" offered Steve, who was aware that something was bothering his friend that he didn't want to discuss in front of Mark.

Colin picked up his drink and wandered over to sit with Steve and Georgia, who were conveniently seated at the opposite side of the room to Mark.

"As I said, it's Mark's birthday soon, and he's told me what he wants as a gift. He's told me that he wants to get an engagement ring for Celia. If he did give her the ring, it would add a whole new level of formally recognising that they intend to get married. The fact is that they are both in their mid-twenties, and as such they have every right to get married, and unless I, or Celia's parents, wish to contest whether they are capable of making such decisions, then we can't stand in their way, and I'm not saying I want to. I had quite a heated exchange of views with my sister-in-law, who says that I should do all in my power to quash any thoughts of marriage. She argued that it was 'unnatural', but I can't accept that. I've watched their relationship grow, and while they've had extra obstacles put in their way, I'm convinced that they are very fond of each other. Quite a number of my friends have commented on how Mark and Celia look good together, but most of the comments seem to be slightly patronising. They say how 'sweet' they are together and that they look 'quite grown up' as if they are just children playing some harmless game that they will tire of soon. The issue isn't taken seriously, and I expect that some people will be genuinely shocked when they find out that it's not just all a game.

"The issue I keep coming back to is whether they are sufficiently in love to commit to being with each other for the rest of their lives. I've talked it over with Celia's parents, who are fortunately more enlightened than my sister-in-law. It was a strange conversation, as though we were contemplating an arranged marriage for our children. While they share my reservations, they admit that they feel their daughter is set on the idea of marrying Mark. I feel I ought to have the courage to declare my support, but I get a niggling doubt that I'd be shirking my responsibilities."

"I suppose that marriage is not the only solution," suggested Georgia. "Steve and I may be getting married someday, but in the meantime we are happy just living together. It's a radical thought, but perhaps if they had some time to live together, they could see if they are really suited?"

"Celia's mother did briefly consider if any domestic arrangements could be arranged to facilitate that, and I have obliquely touched on the subject with Mark, but he is adamant that he wants to get married. He saw how my Jackie and I enjoyed nearly fifty years of marriage, and he sees that as the arrangement he wants. I must admit that I would prefer him to have the relative security of marriage. It's rather ironic that Jackie and I were together for a few years before we decided to get married, but of course, it's never been anything we discussed with Mark. Jackie and I always made a point of talking through any aspect of relationships with Mark at the appropriate times in his life, so he has a reasonably clear idea of the basics of sexual relationships, but I still keep asking myself if he is emotionally ready."

"Steve and I had to make the decision as to whether we wanted to be together, and when it came down to it, we decided that it was the right thing to do because we were in love. It was never a matter as to whether it was domestically or financially beneficial. The fact is that entering into any relationship is always a gamble, as can be shown by the number of failed relationships and marriages that end in divorce, but unless you take the risk, you will never know."

"It was certainly not a decision based on having someone to cook meals and look after the house for me," added Steve provocatively.

"Which is just as well," said Georgia, "or our relationship would have never got off the ground. On a serious note, I can see that such issues need to be thought through. I'm sure that Mark and Celia would need a degree of support if they were living together."

"It's a problem that constantly exercises the mind of any caring parent who has a child who is not going to be able to live totally without that support," said Colin. "Jackie and I explored all sorts of possibilities for Mark. I am aware of the fact that I'm not going to live forever, and my greatest priority now is to sort something out for Mark before I go. We set up a trust in his name to try and ensure that he has financial security, but I want him to have more than just that. Like any good parent, I want him to be happy, and the one thing that he searches for, to secure that happiness, is to be able to share his life with the woman he loves. I don't have any right to stand in the way of that happiness. I know that, but I still have that reluctance to let him go his own way. Perhaps I'm just too protective; after a lifetime of trying to make his life as comfortable as I could, am I denying him the chance to make his own decisions and possibly his own mistakes?"

"Presumably, Celia's parents are having to face up to a similar dilemma?" commented Georgia.

"Yes. Jackie and I got to know the family over the years, and we've often skirted around the subject of our children's futures. As you know, Mark was our only child, rather an unexpected bonus late in life, but Celia has two brothers. Charley is a couple of years older than Celia, and he is married to a girl in Newport, and they have two kids themselves. Josh is a year younger than Celia, and he is fiercely protective of her. He's made it very clear that he doesn't like the idea of her 'playing' at having a boyfriend, and his views have coloured his parent's attitude to their daughter's relationship a bit. Josh had never attended the family socials organised by her school or later by the day centre his sister attended. He accepted that his sister had learning problems, but she looked like any other young girl. Obviously, Mark's Down syndrome meant that he had distinctive features, so if we ever went out, then strangers knew that he might need particular consideration. Celia's family had some awkward times when members of the public didn't realise that some of her behaviour was not simply a sign of bad parenting. Josh still sees his sister as being 'just a bit slow', and I get the impression that he is reluctant to accept that she has quite complex needs. He sees her as 'normal' and assumes that someday she will settle down with someone who is similar."

"I can only guess at how complicated all this is for you, Colin," said Steve before adding, "All I can say is that you've obviously put a great deal of thought into it, and I'm sure that you will do what's right for Mark."

"We do have the benefit of him having a very supportive social worker, and she can't see any reason why the couple shouldn't be together. Appropriate accommodation is rather thin on the ground, but she's more than willing to explore all possibilities. She is conscious of my dilemma and doesn't want to put too much pressure on me, but we both know that the issue can't be shelved indefinitely. I've talked it through with a number of the parents at our local Mencap group. As an organisation, Mencap are committed to showing that people with learning difficulties have the same rights as anyone else to form relationships and to get married if they want to. When it comes down to your own child, there are all sorts of emotional complications, and the issue becomes less clear-cut. The only people who have no reservations about the possible marriage are Mark and Celia."

"And you are sure about what Celia wants?" prompted Georgia.

"I've known her for years, but I wouldn't claim to know how she feels on any subject, but I have seen her with Mark, and they seem to go together well. Her parents also feel that the relationship is a strong one, and she isn't simply 'playing' at boyfriends as her brother suggests."

The small group fell silent for a while, and they all found themselves looking over at Mark and Celia. The young couple were sitting quietly, holding hands, and apparently involved in conversation which caused the occasional shared laughter. They certainly looked content in each other's company, and Mark hadn't once rushed over to tell one of his jokes. He obviously had more important things on his mind. It was a touching scene, and Georgia found herself holding Steve's hand.

"Thanks for listening," said Colin. "It's helped me make up my mind."

"But we haven't really said anything," claimed Georgia.

"It's been helpful to have someone to listen. As I've rumbled through the whole issue in attempting to explain it to you, I've got it a little clearer in my own head. I knew all along that I had no right to stand in the way of their relationship, and when I clarified the picture for you, it became even more apparent to me that I have to try and help them with the next stage in their lives. If my sister-in-law and any like-minded individuals are unhappy about it, they don't need to come to the wedding. All I need to do now is sort the practicalities, and that won't be easy. I'll inform Celia's parents of my commitment. Now that I've come to a decision, I can have a word with them, and the sooner, the better, as it's Mark's birthday soon, and he keeps asking about the engagement ring. I shall see them tomorrow morning; we often meet up on a Sunday for coffee. We all get on well, and it gives Mark and Celia a little time to be together away from the day centre. I'm pretty sure that Celia's parents have come to the same conclusion and will be pleased for us to work together. Then, we can see Mark's social worker about a more definite plan of action."

"And you'll give Mark his birthday money to buy the engagement ring?"

"I certainly will, and it won't be some cheap little thing that's been pulled from a Christmas cracker. This thing's going to be done proper," said Colin as he made to get up to go over and see Mark and Celia.

"Before you go, Colin," said Steve. "Have you been able to discuss Stan's position with Mark's social worker?"

"I managed to grab a few minutes with her at the day centre. She was keen to point out that, contrary to popular opinion, the social services are not keen to take everybody into care. She has some basic information about Stan's position, and while she can't make any official announcement yet, she reiterated that she's pretty sure that there could be some light support given to Stan. She would like to see him remain in his own home, perhaps with someone to call in, as and when needed, to make sure that he was OK."

"That sounds pretty positive," added Georgia. "I'm sure that there are plenty of people who would continue to help Stan, but it would be good to have someone in control, particularly to look after his financial matters. Thanks for putting that word in for us, Colin."

Steve and Georgia watched as Colin walked over to chat with Mark and his soon-to-be fiancée. There was no sudden show of jubilation as Colin had obviously decided to confirm the matter with Celia's parents before letting the young couple know how he felt. There would be no engagement announcement that evening, but it was clear to Steve and Georgia that there would be some celebration soon.

"I was surprised at the way Mike talked so openly today," said Steve, as he remembered the discussion with him in the shed. "But as I said, I think it was because the surroundings were right. Most of us have things we might like to share with others, but the situation has to be conducive. I think that once he started to suspect something about the identity of Stan's mother, he wanted to put out a few ideas as they occurred to him. It was rather like thinking out loud while having someone to listen to his deductions. I've noticed myself that sometimes the need to explain my thinking to someone else means that I have to get it clear in my own head what the issues are, and that helps me better understand how I see the matter. As you know, my mum is a very religious person, and she often claimed that when she prayed, it helped her to better understand her situation. When she felt that she was talking to God, she had to be clear what it was that she was praying for in her discussion with her maker. The very process of planning out her request clarified what she really wanted in her life at that time. As I see it, the thing about prayer is that you don't actually need a response; it just makes you concentrate on the issues that concern you at the time."

CHAPTER ELEVEN

The following day, being Sunday was the one day when Georgia and Steve treated themselves to a cooked breakfast. He enjoyed the ritual of making bacon and eggs and any appropriate accompaniments that he could find in the fridge. He carefully removed the rind from the bacon and cut it into small pieces, which he put into a plastic box which was always in the kitchen to collect any morsels that would suit Stan's friends in the churchyard. Sunday morning was generally a leisurely time, and breakfast was always accompanied by at least two cups of tea.

"I wonder if Colin has met up with Celia's parents yet," mused Steve.

"It's quite an issue to talk through," observed Georgia. "Colin seemed pretty sure that they would all agree to the principle, but that's only the start of it. For a while, Mark would no doubt be delighted to just be engaged, and I'm sure that Celia would feel the same, but after the initial celebrations, decisions would have to be made about where the couple would live when they got married. It will all have to be handled very carefully to manage the young couple's expectations."

"I have to admit that, like most people, I had not thought of Mark actually being serious about wanting to marry Celia. I guess that I'm like so many people who look upon individuals with learning difficulties as not having the same range of needs as the rest of us. I know that I would feel that my life was empty without you. Living with you has only served to deepen my love for you and convinced me that I need to be with you. If we had been restricted to a platonic relationship, I would have felt the whole situation unbearably frustrating, so why should we deny Mark and Celia the opportunity to develop their love if they feel that is what they want? They've been together for a while, and they are obviously extremely happy in each other's company. It's not as if they just woke up one morning and decided to 'play' at being married for a while. We had friends at university who rushed into marriage after a very short time and, unfortunately, some of them ended very quickly."

"Marry in haste and repent at leisure, as the old saying goes," observed Georgia, before adding, "There are 'whirlwind romances' that do stand the test of time, thankfully, but surely it is better to give a lot of thought before deciding with whom you would want to spend the rest of your life. You certainly can't accuse Mark and Celia of rushing into anything. I do hope it works out for them."

As the shop was closed on Sundays, Steve had agreed to help Georgia to do a bit of extra deep cleaning in the back of the display area, and the young couple worked energetically to get the job finished, but it was still after midday before they sat down in the flat to very welcome cups of coffee. Steve looked over at the small plastic container he knew was full of treats for the birds. He had resisted taking it over to the churchyard immediately after breakfast because he knew that the morning service would be going on. While it did not attract the congregation it might have done some years ago, there was still a hard core of parishioners who turned up each Sunday morning, and he didn't want to have a flock of large birds upsetting them.

"I think I'll just nip over with the food for Stan's friends. Do you fancy a walk over?" he asked.

"No. I think I'd rather get on with preparing something for dinner that I can put in the oven later; I thought we might pop down to the Trout after our hard work today."

"A sound proposition. I'll take the bird food over and see if Stan is there."

He picked up the small plastic box of treats, and before leaving, he stopped and kissed her, saying, "I'm glad no one tried to deny us the opportunity to be together, darling."

As he approached the church, he could see no sign of Stan, but Mike was there, standing by the small stone that marked Mary's grave. Steve went over and sat on his usual bench as he didn't want to intrude into what was obviously a contemplative moment for his friend. For the same reason, he resisted the temptation to throw any food out for the birds as their noisy feeding session would disturb the relative tranquillity of the moment. The birds did not fly down in anticipation of food as they might have done if Stan was there. The large birds were slightly more relaxed with Steve around, but they were still not as trusting if Stan wasn't there. After a while, Mike strolled over and took a seat on the bench by Steve. Apart from exchanging simple verbal acknowledgements, the two men sat in silence for a few minutes.

"For all these years, I've wondered what happened to my Mary," said Mike, glancing in the direction of her grave. "I wanted to know why she had left me, and I tried to find her. Now I know what happened to her, I might have expected to have some sense of closure, some satisfaction at having found the answer, but instead of that, I have a gnawing deep sense of despair when I think of what might have been. I want to blame the Falklands, the army, and her bloody mother, but I keep asking myself if I could have done more. I can't escape the feeling that I missed out on all those years I could have been with her. We could have been a real family, but it was all denied us."

"I can't pretend to imagine how you must feel, but what I will say is that you shouldn't start looking to blame yourself. It all happened at a time when you knew absolutely nothing about what was going on with Mary. You did what you could to stay in touch. Nobody could have asked more of you."

"I know the logic of the situation, but it doesn't shift that sense of letting her down. There isn't a lot I can do now, but I'm going to do all I can to support Stan. I know he has to be my son, but even if he weren't, I would do everything I could for him because he's Mary's son, and I would do it for her sake. It's a great pity that I didn't know the situation even after Mary had gone because I would never have let his loathsome grandmother treat him the way she did. The whole thing makes me feel so angry. In my job, I was expected to get things done, to face up to difficult situations, to solve problems, to be active, but when it came to Mary, I was unable to help her at the time. Now I feel powerless to put things right, and it's a sensation that I have great difficulty coping with."

The two men sat in silence for some time, and after a while Stan's friend Paddy flew down and walked around on the ground a few yards from them. His piercing eyes looked out from his shiny black plumage, and he appeared to gaze at the two men with quizzical disapproval as he looked for the treats that he felt ought to be forthcoming from the small plastic box which was on the bench next to Steve. Eventually, the contents were scattered on the ground. Paddy was quick to move in on this bounty, and the sight of him caused some of the crows and rooks to fly off from their vantage points in the high trees that surrounded part of the churchyard. For a few moments, they flew over from one high point to another, all the time keeping an eye on the tempting food below them. Steve knew that if Stan had been there on his own, then the birds would not have displayed such a tentative approach. Eventually, perhaps envious of Paddy getting all the choice morsels or even fearing that he might eat the lot, one adventurous crow flew down. He quickly snatched up a piece from the feast and flew off. It was as if this was a sign for the others to join in, and within seconds the former spread of food was a mass of large birds competing energetically for their share of the banquet before flying off back to the treetops.

"They wouldn't have been so skittish if Stan had been here," commented Mike.

"No. He appears to have a calming effect on them; they are reassured by his presence, but then, he must have spent so much time down here with them over the years. They really have been his friends for so long. I thought he might be up here today."

"He'll be at the pub by now," said Mike. "We have been in the habit of meeting down there at lunchtime some days. It's part of my effort to get to know him a bit more. I wish I'd been around when he was younger, in those golden days before his accident, so he could have let me share the pride of his many successes. I was never close with my father, but I can remember the joy of running back home after school one day to share the news with him that I'd been selected for the county schools football team. I just console myself with the fact that at least I know Stan now, and I'm determined to try and make up a bit for all the missing years. I was on my way to the pub today when I felt that I needed to come and have a word with Mary. I've stood by a lot of graves over the years; it almost went with the job during my army career. I've experienced the loss of close comrades and attended services with full military honours, but nothing compares to the feelings I have when standing next to Mary's unpretentious little plot."

"Did you have any further thoughts on confirming your relationship to Stan?"

"Yes, I got some details from the internet about paternity testing. I don't do all that technical computer stuff, but I met a very helpful young lady in Newport Library who helped me.

You can get access to the internet there, but obviously I had to ask for her help. I lied and said that I was asking on behalf of a friend. She talked me through the search procedures, and within five minutes I had the address of a firm who would do the testing. I wrote to the company, enclosing the required funding, and they will send me two kits. When I get them, I shall do the necessary mouth swab and then get Stan to do the other. I've spoken to the social worker who's currently acting to support Stan, and she has agreed to act on his behalf to consent to the test. I don't want to confuse him with the purpose of the procedure. I'll tell him it's just a routine medical test, which in a way it is, and then send the two kits off for comparison."

"I guess you'll have to wait a while for the results. I know they did with the DNA samples linked to Brad Carter's incident."

"No. In fact, if the samples arrive at the laboratory before 10.00, I could have the results back with me the next day. I have to be honest and admit that I didn't want to rush through the tests because I know that, until the results come through, I'm convinced that they will show I'm Stan's dad. But there is that niggling doubt which means that there is part of me that doesn't want to know. The kits should arrive early in the week, and I know that I really do have to get them off quickly. Once I've got Stan's sample, I shall send them off and should have the results before next weekend."

"Wow! It's going to be quite a week as you wait for the results, but it will be good to get the whole thing settled. What will you do once you have the proof you need?"

"I don't know exactly what my plans will be. It seems such a massive issue for me, and I feel quite overwhelmed at the prospect of having to deal with the results."

"And, assuming the tests are positive, how will you tell Stan?"

"I honestly don't know," admitted Mike. "I've mentally rehearsed it, but the truth is that I'll just have to make it up as I go along and see how Stan reacts. At the back of my mind is that horrible little doubt that I'm not his dad, and I think that by planning ahead too much, I'm somehow tempting fate. Anyway, I'll deal with it in due course, but for now I'd better get down to the Trout to meet him."

Steve sat for a while, just enjoying the peace of the churchyard in the warm afternoon sun. The birds had all flown off, presumably to their next feeding points for the day. For a while, he considered the mental turmoil that Mike was facing as he faced up to the truth that would come with the test results, and then his thoughts turned to the situation that Mark and Celia's parents were having to cope with. Parenting was obviously a tricky business. It was more than a few happy years spent playing with children; parenting was for life and not just for the satisfaction of watching your offspring enjoying a few childhood Christmases. He had often been told that Christmas was for children, but some people didn't recognise that children were not just for Christmas.

He wondered for a moment if he and Georgia would raise a family someday; he had rarely considered it before, and they had never discussed it. It was this thought that made him aware that he ought to, no wanted, to get back to the shop to see her. Their immediate future was uncertain, but it was one that was full of opportunities. They would no doubt have their share of hardship in their lives together, but he felt confident that their love would get them through the hard times, and he couldn't wait to get back to be with her. With all the emotional turmoil going on in the lives of those around him, he once again experienced a deep sense of gratification at the way his and Georgia's entwined lives were developing. Being in love, and more importantly, being in a loving relationship, suddenly felt particularly good.

The Trout was rather busy that evening as Steve and Georgia arrived.

"Good evening," Tony greeted them. "You look rather pleased with yourselves. I guess you must be pretty happy about the job offer, Steve?"

"Yes, we are both pleased, and we've been determined to celebrate," he said, glancing covertly at Georgia. He didn't bother to ask how Tony knew about the job offer; after all, this was a village and news spread quickly through the local grapevine. What Steve didn't elaborate on was the fact that their celebrations had involved a rather romantic afternoon together, and it was this, rather than his improved career situation, that had induced the current sense of contentment that they both radiated.

"Mike and Stan were in at lunchtime, and Mike was saying that he had seen you at the church. That pair seem to get on very well with each other these days, and Stan is at last being able to enjoy life a bit; he was even laughing at times, and that's been a rare sight for the last few years."

Their conversation was dramatically interrupted by the arrival of Mark, who almost danced up to the bar, hand-in-hand with Celia, followed by his dad, who was obviously a bit embarrassed at his son's exuberance.

"I'm going to have an engagement party," blurted out Mark before looking at Celia and clarifying, "My fiancée and me are going to have a party."

Throughout this announcement, Celia stood quietly, smiling coyly while Mark held on to her hand as if to ensure that nobody could take her from him.

"That's wonderful news," declared Georgia, stepping forward and kissing Mark and then Celia. "So when is the party to be held?"

"On my birthday," Mark announced proudly.

"And when is that?" asked Steve.

"That's what I had hoped to discuss before my son's public announcement," answered Colin, almost apologetically as he turned to Tony. "I was hoping that we could have a little do here, like the birthday events you put on for Mark's friends from the day centre. They both wanted to meet up here. I don't want it to be the biggest society event of the year, but they both feel comfortable here, and it would be good for them to have something special to celebrate the event."

"We would be honoured," replied a delighted Tony. "I'll call Monica through from the back in a minute, and you can have a word with her, and she'll sort it all out. In the meantime, I'm sure the happy couple would like a celebratory drink."

Taking Mark's exotic martini and a coke for Celia, the couple made their way to their usual seats, where they sat holding hands and occasionally giggling. In the meantime, Colin joined Georgia and Steve at another table.

"I had hoped to try and avoid that display," explained Colin. "But when he heard that he could have an engagement ring for Celia, he wanted to shout it from the rooftops. Judging by the crowd in here tonight, the whole village will know about it by tomorrow, but I would guess that most of them will think that it's just Mark being his old self."

"We can understand his excitement," said Georgia. "When we decided that we wanted to be together, I wanted everyone to share in our happiness. I gather the meeting went well with Celia's parents this morning?"

"Yes. I think they were relieved that I had brought the matter up first and that I had shown my support for the engagement. None of us are naïve enough to think that we have sorted the whole matter. We all have reservations about whether or not we have done the right thing. We don't want our children to be hurt, but we would be doing them a great disservice if we denied them the chance to experience all that life can offer. At times, it will no doubt be difficult, but for the moment they are on their own little cloud nine. Celia had hoped that her parents would be able to come over tonight and give her a bit of moral support, but they have arranged to have a family meeting to discuss Celia's future. I don't envy them. Their eldest son will no doubt see the decision as being fine, but I suspect young Josh will take some convincing. He still sees Celia as some kind of pretty little doll that needs protecting from the harsh reality of relationships. He apparently can't accept that she's a young woman who wants to choose her own course in life. I know that my sister-in-law will be alarmed that I am respecting Mark's wishes to take charge of his own life, and I know that there will be others who will disagree with my decision. I think that some of the locals are quite prepared to smile at Mark's talk about getting married, but will they be quite as pleased when they see that he is serious about it?"

"There are always going to be people who will be reluctant to accept the fact that individuals who might have obvious differences can still experience the normal range of emotions," added Steve.

"A lot of it comes down to the old issue of prejudice," suggested Colin. "We all have our own little prejudices. Whenever we meet anyone new, we have a tendency to want to fit them in some kind of memory box so that we can recall them later. The trouble is that we tend to assume that all people in a particular box are the same, and we can be quick to resort to stereotypes. I have an old friend called Morgan who is Welsh, so he goes in the Welsh box in my memory chest along with all the associated attributes of 'Welshness'; he must be able to play rugby, eat leeks and, above all, have a fine operatic voice. I know nothing about Morgan's preference for vegetables, but I know that he hates rugby and has the singing voice of a strangulated duck. It's only when we start to examine the assumptions that we make about people that we see how ridiculous they can be.

"Unfortunately, many people will just see Mark and Celia as being two people with special needs, and they will go into the memory chest among any other people who might have similar conditions, so the label becomes what they *are*. I don't want to appear too critical because Celia's parents and I have also had to come to terms with our prejudices about our own children. It's a sad fact that many people are reluctant to ever question the assumptions they make about others. Life is simpler if you make up your mind about someone before you have a full understanding of what they are like. A well-established prejudice does away with the need to think."

Their conversation was interrupted by the appearance of Monica from behind the bar, who had obviously heard the news about the proposed engagement party. She went over to Mark and Celia, smiling broadly, and kissed them both in turn. It was obvious that she was delighted at the news, and her obvious elation probably went some way to convincing some of the customers in the pub that this was not just Mark acting out one of his fantasies. After spending a few minutes chatting with the young couple, Monica came over to talk with Colin.

"That is the best news I've had in a long time," she said. "I must admit that I was a bit surprised because Mark has been talking about his 'fiancée' for as long as he's been coming in here. We will of course be delighted to put on some sort of party if you can give us some idea of how many guests you might expect and the date you have in mind. There's no rush."

"That could be complicated," replied Colin. "There will probably be the usual crowd from the day centre, but I will just have to see how some of our friends respond to the idea of

Mark and Celia getting married. We've already come across a couple of family members who are unhappy that Celia's parents and I are 'encouraging' the wedding. The truth is that we are not encouraging it, but rather recognising that the young couple are serious about wanting to be together. We have no right, legally or morally, to stand in their way."

While this conversation was going on, at the other side of the bar, Mark and Celia had been chatting, or rather, Mark had been chatting, and Celia had been listening. It had long been realised that he was the more dynamic member of the partnership, while Celia was content to play a more sedate role. She was naturally quiet and a little bit on the shy side, but she was still more than capable of making her views heard when she wanted to. After a short while, holding firmly onto Celia's hand, Mark approached his father's group.

"I have some jokes for my speech," he announced to a less than impressed audience. "What's orange and sounds like a parrot?" he asked.

"A carrot," answered Celia promptly, thus effectively denying Mark his own dramatic answer, but he was determined not to be upstaged.

"What's black, white and blue?" he continued.

"A sad zebra," came back Celia's immediate response before she went on to make a suggestion. "We don't need too many jokes at the party, do we?"

"Perhaps you should just thank people for turning up and say how happy you both are and save one of your best jokes to tell everyone?" offered Georgia.

Colin smiled as he listened to Celia's comments. It was clear that she was not the submissive little girl she might appear to be, who was prepared to just be dominated by her future husband. She had a gentle strength that ensured that she would be an equal partner in the relationship, and Colin was pleased to see it. As the evening progressed, some of the customers went over to see Mark and Celia, and it was clear that a number of them were congratulating the couple on their news.

"It's reassuring to see that some of the locals appear to be taking the engagement seriously," commented Colin. "I had feared that there would be a reluctance to accept the news as genuine. Celia's parents and I are under no illusions as to the fact that there will be some who will find it difficult to recognise that Mark and Celia are right for each other and deserve the right to get married, but then, you can't please everyone."

"Mark seems even happier than he usually is," observed Georgia. "And Celia appears to have come out of her shell a bit; she seems to be glowing with happiness. They certainly look very happy together."

CHAPTER TWELVE

Some days later, Steve arrived home to find Mike chatting to Georgia and Rita in the shop. He joined in with the conversation, and for a while they discussed how things were going at the factory and other such small talk. Eventually, having finished her shift, Rita put on her coat, wished everyone goodbye, and left.

"I'm sorry to bother you this evening," said Mike, "I couldn't mention it in front of Rita, but I've had the results from the DNA tests."

"I thought there might be something else," said Steve. "So, how did it go?"

"The results are absolutely clear. Stan is my son."

"That's wonderful," declared Georgia as she hugged Mike.

"Fantastic news," added Steve as he shook the older man's hand vigorously.

"I wanted to tell someone; I'm just so happy about the outcome. I haven't told Stan anything yet. The truth is that I've been going out of my way not to bump into him since I got the letter this morning. I want to find the right time and place to tell him rather than to see him in the street and just casually mention that I'm his dad. It seems stupid to think that, during my career, I experienced all sorts of harrowing events, and yet now I'm scared to death of facing up to my own son and explaining who I am. I guess I'm just worried sick about how he will respond. Part of it is that I don't know just how much he will understand. In a way, the tests also prove that I was right to maintain that Mary would have had no other partners around that time. I almost felt a sense of guilt taking the test because it may have suggested that I doubted her, but the results vindicate her as well."

"I'm sure that Stan will welcome the idea once he comes to terms with the information. It's quite obvious that you get on very well together, so your relationship doesn't need to dramatically change. I've seen you sitting with him in the churchyard and in the pub, and you look like father and son already."

"How does this affect your legal position?" asked Georgia, who had begun to consider the issues concerning Stan's domestic arrangements and the fact that the social services had been approached to look into his long-term future.

"I've been reading the letter I got this morning. To be honest, I've read it over and over again because I can hardly believe my luck. It states that the two samples definitely show a father-son relationship, but it also says that the document would not be accepted in a court of law. To make it legal, we would have to pay extra for another test under specific conditions to confirm the results, presumably to prove the samples came from Stan and me. I'll do that if I ever need to, but in the meantime, I've got to decide how to tell Stan."

Mike stayed for a while, obviously delighted to share the good news with his friends, but eventually he set off home.

"That's fantastic news," observed Georgia after Mike had left. "I know he's been secretly worried that the results might not have been what he wanted to hear. The more you think about it, the more obvious it was that they were related, but I know how much he had invested emotionally in the issue, and there was always that slim possibility that he wasn't Stan's dad, but it's all sorted now; except for the small matter of telling Stan. I assumed it would have been a wonderful moment for

Mike to be able to announce the news to Stan, but it's obviously not that simple. It would be a shock for anyone to suddenly hear that one of their friends is, in fact, their father, and there is the added complication of wondering just how much Stan would understand."

"Mike's obviously worried about how the news will be received," commented Steve, "but we'll all just have to wait and see how things turn out."

The following Saturday morning, Steve picked up the box of scraps for the birds and wandered over to the churchyard, where he found Stan sitting on his regular bench. Unless there were any specific jobs that the vicar wanted doing, Stan no longer went to the church every day and tended to have the weekends off. His gran was no longer there to chase him out from the house every morning, so he kept his weekends for leisure, although he still went up to the church just to sit and spend a little time with his animal friends. On this particular day, Steve noted that Stan seemed somewhat different, almost morose, and Steve wondered if he had reacted badly to the special news Mike might have passed on to him.

"Morning Stan," said Steve. "You don't seem your usual self today. Aren't you feeling too good?"

"It was the sad news."

Steve was momentarily taken aback by this reply. Why should Stan be so upset by hearing about his parentage? In an attempt to introduce a lighter tone to the conversation, he changed the subject.

"I've brought some treats for your friends."

Stan took the small box but did not immediately put it out to attract his friends.

"Bad news. Not fair. Shouldn't do that."

Steve realised that he couldn't avoid whatever was upsetting his friend and felt obliged to delve a little deeper.

"It's just the way things are, Stan. We can't change it. Things will work out well in the end."

"Not for the dog, it's not fair. He didn't mean it."

Belatedly, Steve realised that there was some obvious confusion over what was being discussed, and he tried to clarify just what Stan was talking about.

"What news did you get this morning, Stan?"

"On the television news this morning. A dog attacked a man who had tried to hit him with a stick. The man was in hospital, but the dog had to be killed for what he did. Not fair. He was a nasty man. Dog didn't mean it."

"I'm sure they wouldn't have put the dog down unless it was a serious attack or if it had a history of attacking people. We don't know all the details. It's sad that an animal should have to be destroyed, but perhaps it was justified. If animals attack people, then it's a very serious matter."

The couple sat for a few minutes before Stan opened the box of bird treats and scattered them on the floor. Paddy was quick to appear, followed by a couple of crows and some rooks, who quickly cleared up the food. Stan had kept a particularly choice bit of meat aside, and he put it on the arm of the bench. Within seconds, Paddy was there helping himself to his special reward. Stan smiled at the bird, which hung around for a few minutes with his prize in his beak before flying off. The interlude had obviously taken his mind off the death of the dog, and his mood was improved further by the arrival of Mike, who joined them on the bench. After exchanging greetings, the three men sat in silence, looking out over the gravestones. Steve seemed pretty sure that Mike had not broken his particular piece of news to Stan, and his suspicion was proven right when Mike started talking about the arrangements for putting gravestones out for Mary and her mother. There was nothing in what he said that might imply that he had broached the subject of Stan's parentage.

"There is something that I need to talk to you about, lad," started the older man. Steve took this as a good point to leave the two men alone, but as he discreetly got up to leave, Mike encouraged him to stay.

"No. Don't go, Steve. You're a friend of Stan's, and it might be useful to have someone with him."

Mike said nothing for a while, and then, turning to Stan, he imparted his news.

"You remember that you did that medical test with the little cotton bud inside your mouth, and I sent it away?"

"Yes, it was a funny test. Tickled."

"Well, that test showed certain things." Mike paused for some seconds before hesitantly continuing, "I had a girlfriend called Mary, and the test that I did showed that we had a baby. Your test shows that you were that baby. Your mother Mary was my girlfriend."

For a while, Mike left Stan time to take in this dramatic news, but it was obvious that the younger man had not grasped the implication of this revelation, so Mike put it in the most simple terms.

"I'm your dad, Stan."

In the ensuing lengthy silence, Mike and Steve sat apprehensively and awaited Stan's response as he slowly mulled over the information he was being gradually fed.

"Dad? My dad? Gran said I didn't have a dad."

"I know it's strange. Until a few days ago, I didn't know that Mary had a baby. I didn't know I had a son, or I would have been here for you all along. Your gran knew all about me, but she didn't want me to marry your mum."

"You're my dad? Gran didn't tell me. You're really my dad?"

"I am. The tests we did prove that I'm your dad."

"How do you feel about Mike being your father, Stan?" ventured Steve.

"Really, my dad? I never had a dad before. It's good to have a dad."

"I never had a son before," added Mike. "And it's good to have a son."

"How do you feel about celebrating this new-found relationship, Mike?" asked Steve. "We could go down to the Trout later, but you'd have to be prepared for the entire village to have got the news by this time tomorrow."

"I think that's a great idea. Now I've got the proof, and I know Stan is up for accepting me as his dad, I want everyone to know, so why don't we arrange to meet down at the pub at six this evening?"

Steve left the two men talking about their newly confirmed relationship and made his way back to the shop to tell Georgia how things had gone. She was busy serving a customer when he arrived, and he waited impatiently while the transaction was completed and they were on their own.

"Mike just told Stan about the results of the tests," he announced.

"And how did it go? Did Stan seem happy about the situation?"

"He certainly seemed so, but I'm not sure how much of it he grasped. Anyone who suddenly finds that they have a father that they knew nothing about is bound to find it a bit of a shock, but in Stan's case, it is hard to know just how much he has understood. After years of his gran telling him that he had a 'good-for-nothing father', he now finds that the man he has grown to like as his friend is that same person."

"His gran has a lot to answer for. She seemed capable of screwing up the lives of everybody she came in contact with, and even now that she's gone, her evil influence continues to cause waves."

The Trout was reasonably empty at six that evening when Georgia and Steve turned up, but Stan and Mike were already sitting with their drinks at one of the tables while Tony was moving some clean glasses around behind the bar in preparation for the evening's session.

Steve and Georgia collected a drink from the bar and joined their friends.

"Have you told anyone else, Mike?" asked Georgia.

"No. I just can't decide on the best way to approach the topic. It's not as if such things would naturally crop up in conversation. I even briefly thought of making an announcement in the parish magazine."

"No need to do that," commented Steve. "Even with my limited understanding of the area, I know that you just have to let Mrs Holland at the post office know about it, and the whole village would know before the day was out."

"I know," said the older man, "but I don't want it to be a big announcement. I was chuffed to bits to get the letter, and I want everyone to share my good news."

"Had some good news then, Mike?" commented Tony who had been innocently collecting a couple of used glasses from a nearby table.

Mike realised that he had to make an instant decision as to how much he should disclose about his relationship to Stan. A simple announcement that Stan was his son seemed rather abrupt, so he decided to give some of the background. If the matter was disclosed, then people ought to have some indication as to how the issue had become apparent and how it had been proven.

"It's all been a rather tangled story, Tony. In a nutshell, I had a very dear girlfriend, Mary, in the village here, but I was called away at short notice by the army and we were split up. All my efforts to contact my girl were fruitless. Recently, I found that my girlfriend had a baby that I knew absolutely nothing about."

"And Stan was that baby?" interrupted Tony.

"Yes, but how did you know?"

"I didn't know, but when you started talking about someone called Mary having a baby, and I recalled all the gossip about who could have been Mary Truelove's secret lover, it seemed a strong possibility. Added to that, having seen the way that you obviously get on so well with Stan, it seemed a reasonable assumption."

"We only found out ourselves recently," continued Mike. "An old photograph, a diary entry and some elementary mathematics meant that Steve, Georgia and I were pretty certain of our conclusion, so I arranged for one of those clever DNA tests and it proved we were right. All those years that I tried to get in contact with her and all the heartache because I thought she didn't want to know me, and I find her evil mother was destroying all the letters I sent."

"Well, congratulations to the pair of you. I think this warrants a round of drinks," offered Tony. "But before I get them in, how do you wish your recent news to be handled?"

"I've been chewing over that little issue for days," admitted Mike. "But now that the first little trickle of news is out, I think we should let the grapevine do the rest. As I said, I want everyone to share our good news."

Tony wandered off to sort out some drinks, but not before he had made a quick visit to the back room of the pub. He emerged with Monica, and they soon came over with a tray of drinks. Monica immediately went over to Mike and Stan and kissed them in turn while congratulating them on their good news. It was apparent that the 'trickle' of information was on its way around the village.

"That's great news," declared Monica. "When I look at the pair of you now, it seems obvious that you are related, but it's still a bit of a shock. How do you feel about your new dad, Stan?"

Stan sat as he tried to work out how best to respond to what might have seemed a simple question but which, in reality, caused him quite a deal of confusion.

"It's good to have a dad. Never had a dad before."

"And you've got more than a dad," Mike reminded his son. "You've got your aunts, uncles and cousins, and even a granddad. All my relatives are part of your family now."

Stan was obviously still having to come to terms with the fact that he was now part of a family. He said very little, but his contented smile showed that he was very happy about his new status, and over the next few days, he took an obvious delight in letting people know about his new family. The news was generally well received, and in particular, many people were pleased to see that Stan had a more stable position within the community, and the possibility of him being persuaded to move to a residential home outside the village diminished. Some villagers, as expected, declared that they had always suspected that Mike was Stan's father. Twenty-twenty hindsight is a wonderful thing.

CHAPTER THIRTEEN

It was a Friday in late August when Steve finished his last shift at the factory. He was due to start working for the water company on the following Monday morning. He wasn't sad to get away from the hard physical work, but he had made some good friends in his time there. On his way home in Don's car, they compared notes on what the immediate future had to offer.

"So, you've managed to escape," commented Don. "I've been able to secure an extra three weeks' employment before I go back to the relative ease of university life, and I'll be glad of the money. What do you know about your new job?"

"Not a lot really. I start at 9.00 on Monday morning, and I've been told that I will be 'shadowing' Denise, the woman that I'm due to take over from. She's been promoted to another regional post. She seems very pleasant, and I get the impression that she's well respected in the company, so she'll be a hard act to follow, but I must admit that I'm up for the challenge."

"And where will you be working?"

"Initially, I will be based in Newport, but a lot of my work will be in the nature reserve in Hartbridge to begin with."

"I thought you were working for the water company."

"I am. The company have responsibility for all aspects of water purity in the district, so they monitor what is going on in the natural water courses in the area. It's got a lot to do with environmental balance, or that's what the job description tells me. To be honest, I don't know exactly what I will be doing to start with, and the job could develop in any one of a number of areas. It's both exciting and a bit scary, but I can't wait to get started."

"Has Georgia had any luck finding a post yet?"

"Nothing concrete, but she sent off an application to the local museum service, so we'll see if anything comes of that."

When Don dropped him off outside the shop, Steve stood for a moment in his work jeans and sweatshirt and reflected on the fact that he would have to dress a bit more formally in his new job. He was about to enter a new phase in his life. He smiled to himself and went in to greet Georgia.

"The worker is home from his toil," he announced melodramatically. "Did you miss me?"

"It was hell without you, but I got by," she responded with a marked lack of sincerity. "But my day was brightened by the letter that arrived this afternoon. It's over there on the counter."

Steve walked over, picked up a brightly coloured envelope and carefully removed what turned out to be a card. On reading the contents, he saw that it was an invitation to an engagement party at the pub. The card had obviously been neatly printed out, giving the time and venue of the party, and at the bottom, it had been signed, in somewhat large print, by Mark and Celia.

"That's one social event that I wouldn't want to miss," observed Steve. "They've obviously gone to some lengths to do this formally, so we must write back and accept. I know we could just tell them we'd like to go, but I think they might value a formal acceptance delivered through the post. In the meantime, we could just let Colin know that we intend to go."

"It will be interesting to see who is invited," added Georgia, "and also to find out who turns up and who attends when it comes to the wedding."

"It's some consolation to know that Mark won't be offended if someone decides not to attend, but I think Celia might be disappointed if her brother chooses not to be there. I suspect that the prospect of Mark and Celia getting married will divide opinion among their friends and relatives. It would be much simpler if they just chose to live together, but Mark's having none of that."

As Steve lay in bed on the following Monday morning, he reflected on the fact that he had not slept well. It was probably because he was emotionally geared up to face the first day in his new job. He only knew that he had woken up several times during the night. Initially, he had felt a deep sense of satisfaction that he could watch Georgia sleeping peacefully beside him, but then his mind started on a rambling assortment of subjects. Obviously, he wondered what his new job would be like; he had briefly met his co-worker and he felt sure that they would get on well, but he still felt some slight apprehension about how he would settle in. Having reassured himself of this, it was as if his brain now wanted something else to examine. At various times during the night, he had found himself wondering how Mike and Stan would settle into their new roles. No sooner had this issue been considered than he would find that he was musing over how Mark and Celia's future together would pan out. With all this mental turmoil, it was hardly surprising that what he could remember of his dreams was rather confusing. He partly recalled an impression of being late for a party, and when he got there, he found himself congratulating Mark and Celia on their wedding. The other party-goers were all members of the village, but what he found strange was the fact that Brad Carter was there, but nobody seemed to mind. In his dream, he had tried to convince people that Brad should not be there, but nobody cared.

As he lay in bed that morning, watching the bedside clock and calculating when he ought to get up, it was the dream that largely occupied his mind. Why had the obnoxious Brad made an appearance? The only sort of conclusion he could come to was that Brad's disappearance had never been explained, so there had been no opportunity for what is enigmatically called 'closure'. Brad had played a major role in village life, and then he had just been removed in some way. While it was true to say that no one missed him, it still left a sense of mystery, an indefinable feeling of unfinished business.

Steve was aware that Georgia was waking up, and he turned to look at her.

"I was just wondering," he began.

"Well, don't bother; we haven't got time. You've got work today."

"For once, despite your undeniable attractive qualities, I was thinking about something else. I was wondering what actually happened to Carter. Every time there is a rumour that a body has been found, I wonder if it's him. I actually saw him in a dream last night."

"How horrible for you. I guess we all have to assume he's dead after the evidence was found by the bridge, but I know what you mean; there is that fear that he might return. Every time I walk down by the river and look over at the mobile home site, I see his empty caravan and his truck is still there. It's as if he could just turn up some time and move back in."

"Well, I haven't got time to think about it now, and despite your protestations and ill-concealed attempts to tempt me to stay, I have a job to go to. As you so wisely pointed out on a previous occasion, it would not be a good career move to pull a sickie on my first day. You'll just have to wait until I get home this evening."

"It's a cross I'll have to bear, but in the meantime, if you put the kettle on, I'll join you for breakfast."

As he stood in the doorway of the shop in some of his smarter clothes and grasping his lunchbox, Georgia insisted on taking a picture of him.

"You look as if you're in one of those classic photos that parents take as their child is about to set off for the first day of school," she said with a slight giggle.

"I feel a bit like that, but they did ask me to be reasonably smart for the first few days of my induction. Once I know where I will be working, I will possibly have to dress differently; I don't want to be crawling about on muddy river banks in these clothes."

"Did you get any insight about your new job from the company blurb that you were reading through?"

"It seems a pretty extensive brief. The water company are very concerned about their public image and their effect on environmental issues. When I applied for the post, I rather naively thought that it was just about getting water into houses and businesses. The fact is that the company take about half of the water they purify from surface sources such as rivers, lakes and reservoirs, so it's in their interests to ensure that all such water is kept in good health. I gather that my role will be to liaise with all sorts of other bodies who all have an interest in keeping the waterways in good shape. One day, I could be working alongside the Environmental Agency, and next I could be alongside a nature conservancy group or the RSPB. You needn't worry about the prospect of me sitting in a lab in a white coat all day; a lot of the work would appear to be very 'hands-on', and I honestly don't know what to expect."

"Never mind, love; just don't let any of the big boys and girls bully you in the playground," she said, patting him on the head.

"Thank you for that much-appreciated advice on how to cope with my first day; I feel much better now and ready to single-handedly ensure that the water you get when you turn on the tap is wholesome and free from bugs."

"Thank you, my hero. I hope that your day goes well."

He kissed her gently and turned to go before turning back and giving her a more meaningful kiss. "I'll see you this evening. I should be back about five, assuming that I cope with the day over by the nature reserve. It's a jungle out there." This last remark was accompanied by a dramatic gesture as he posed with the back of his raised hand to his forehead before manfully striding off to his day's toil.

Steve crossed the road and set off towards the bridge, resisting the temptation to cut through the churchyard. He thought that Stan might be there, and he couldn't afford the time to stand and chat this morning. As he crossed the bridge, he passed the point where Brad Carter had last been seen and, not for the first time, it made him wonder just what had taken place on that spot. There was no time to stand and ponder, so he strode on over the bridge and turned right, passing through a gate indicating that he was entering a nature reserve. The track passed through an extensive area of reeds that bordered the river, and to his left he saw a large area of open water, beside which was a wooden chalet with a sign indicating that it was the property of the water company. Steve entered what was effectively an office and was met by Denise. She was dressed very smartly in a dark business suit, a royal blue blouse and high heels. Steve felt seriously under-dressed but she soon put him at his ease.

"I'm sorry about this, Steve; I know that we had planned for you to follow me around today, but I've been called in to head office. It appears that I've drawn the short straw and have to attend a meeting with the local MP, hence the glad rags. Apparently, someone has been complaining about water being removed from a local river without the appropriate permission, and I've been nominated to explain exactly what we have been doing about it. Apparently, the MP finds it easier to work with women. The truth is that he's a lecherous old goat, but if I just sit around and look girly, he will soon be placated. It's not something I particularly like doing, but it is generally accepted that our Chairman, Sir William Hargreaves, looks less than attractive in a short skirt. Anyway, enough of my troubles. As I have to fly off at such short notice, I've asked Bert to take you under his wing for a while. Bert has been with the company since before water was invented, and you could do worse than listen to what he has to say."

Perfectly on cue, the door was opened by an elderly man dressed in an old camouflage suit and heavy boots.

"Morning, Bert, this is Steve. He'll be taking over from me soon."

The older man looked Steve up and down before giving his considered response.

"Nice to meet you, Steve, but if I can make one observation from the start, I don't think that you should allow them to make you wear a short skirt. The mud gets everywhere, and high heels are generally not a good idea in the marshes either."

"Thanks for displaying your usual respect for my position in the firm, Bert. I'll leave you to get to know each other. There is just a chance that I might be able to get back later this afternoon, but I shouldn't bet on it."

With this announcement, she picked up her attaché case and car keys before rushing off to her day in the world of corporate diplomacy. Bert and Steve stood for a moment in an awkward silence. Steve had felt under-dressed when he had met Denise, but now he felt decidedly too formal alongside Bert.

"What do we do first?" asked Steve.

"I think a cup of tea is always a good start; you'll find all the necessary equipment in the kitchen area through the back there. I take milk and two sugars. While you do that, I'll get out of some of this clobber, and then we can run through some of the work we do here."

Steve dutifully set about making the tea in a rather ancient brown teapot that he found at the back of a cupboard and brought it out with cups, milk and sugar and put them on a short table which was surrounded by a number of comfortable chairs in what was obviously a visitors' reception area. Meanwhile, Bert had discarded his outer camouflage suit to reveal olive green trousers and matching tee shirt. The entire ensemble had obviously seen years of service and was best described as comfortable rather than smart.

"My word, we are going posh today, using the old teapot," said Bert.

"Shall I be mother?" asked Steve, lifting the pot towards Bert's cup.

"Not if you want me to be the gynaecologist," replied the older man.

Steve had no time to respond to this quip before Bert started his home-spun tutorial.

"Well, Steve, my lad, I will give you a rundown on some of our basic duties here, but first things first, what drew you into this area of work?"

"I finished at university this summer and was looking for some employment. I have to admit that I never grew up with a burning ambition to work for a water company, but I saw the advert for this post, and it intrigued me. My degree was in marine biology, and the references to conservation work in the local rivers and lakes seemed to be something that I could enjoy doing."

"Didn't you ever think of going into a job that would pay more? You can see that even after years in this field, I don't dress in fancy clothes, and you can rest assured that I don't have any off-shore investment accounts."

"My partner Georgia and I have never felt that earning a lot of money was the most important thing in life. I must admit that I initially only wrote off to ask about the post because it was important that one of us secured paid work pretty soon, but when I read the job description, I was quite excited at the prospect of coming into this field. So, what brought you into this job?"

"I've had a variety of jobs all over the world. I ran a bar in the Polish quarter in Havana when I was a young man, and then I was recruited by the CIA. They were still a bit miffed about the Bay of Pigs invasion and wanted my inside view on the position because I knew Castro pretty well, as he frequently dropped into my bar for the odd glass of sweet sherry. I worked with the agency for a few years before I did ten years as a stuntman in Hollywood. I was prescribed painkillers for all the injuries I suffered, which led to an addiction problem, and my work fell off, and I was sacked. I went into what I call my 'wilderness years' and resorted to taking any work that I could get, from school janitor to male stripper. After a few years on skid row, I was helped out by an old school friend who got me this post. OK, it doesn't pay as much as my CV might reasonably have been expected to command, but I'm happy enough."

"Fascinating!" exclaimed Steve as he looked at the dishevelled old man in front of him and mentally struggled to decide which part of this story, if any, was, in fact, the truth.

Bert smiled before continuing, "Well, that's how I remember it, but some of the details are a little hazy. I put it down to the painkillers."

The two men sat for quite some time as Bert explained the routines of the job.

"We have a diary in which we record what we have done and what needs to be done. Assignments set in the diary for a particular day might not get done on the assigned day, but we get round to them when we have a chance. Nothing is entirely predictable; if the river overflows into the marshes here, then we might be unable to do what we had planned. We do what we can when we can."

"And what do you see as our main job?" asked Steve, sipping his tea.

"We monitor what is going on and then carry out any work we can to keep the whole thing ticking over. Young people nowadays talk about protecting ecosystems and environmental issues, but in my day we just said we were nature watchers. Everything in nature has a balance; things that grow, things that eat things that grow and other things in turn which eat them. If something upsets the balance, then it affects the whole system. Part of our job is to monitor what the scientists call 'non-native species'. They are things that have been introduced to our part of the world that really don't belong here. It could be a plant or an animal that upsets the balance. We have teams from two local universities who visit regularly to do testing, and we keep them informed of what we record."

"Sounds interesting."

"It gets very technical as they talk about the way chemical pollution can affect microbes in the water and how they can measure DNA stuff to tell what is going on in there. I don't even pretend to understand what they are talking about half the time, but they are a nice bunch of kids, and they like to hear what I have to tell them about what I have observed going on in the wider arena of the marshes. We're on the same side; we all care about what is happening in our world."

"I know what you mean," added Steve. "We did a fieldwork study at a small coastal village in Yorkshire in our last year at university. I knew all sorts about the biological structure of a range of shellfish because it was part of my thesis work, but the local fishermen knew so much more about how the creatures lived and interacted. It was quite a chastening experience to recognise that we students didn't know it all. I, for one, certainly gained a great deal from the locals."

The morning seemed to pass quickly as the older man gave Steve the beginnings of an insight into the complexities of his job and the geography of the nature reserve. Steve was surprised at the size of the wetland area. At one point, Bert had taken him through the extensive reed bed that bordered the river, and they had stood and looked out over the water at the south bank. Steve was surprised to see that he was standing virtually opposite the playing field next to the Trout.

"I hadn't realised that we were so close to the village pub, Bert. I'm surprised that I've never seen you in there."

"No. I rarely go over the water. I live out on the Callerthorpe road, and when I finish work here, I tend to go straight home. My wife, Gina, claims that I almost live down here, so I daren't pop over for a pint and give her more to get at me with. You know what these show business people are like."

"Show business? Your wife is in show business?"

"You wouldn't recognise her in any of her bigger parts. I met her during my time in Hollywood. She spent years as a stunt double for Arnold Schwarzenegger; she's a big girl, so I don't like to upset her by getting home late. She's quite a romantic really, and insists that when I leave home every morning I have to reassure her 'I'll be back'. It's just one of our silly little routines."

"How sweet," commented Steve, who was quite at a loss as to how he should respond to such a comment. Bert certainly had his whimsical side, but he soon snapped back into his role as instructor to his new young friend.

"You can see how dense the reeds are along here, and they extend out into the margins of the river. After extensive rain, all manner of items can be caught up in here as the water spills over and drains down towards the wetland area."

"You mean a body could be swept in here and get trapped in the reeds?"

"Yes, in theory, but I've never had an actual body. We get the odd dead bird or cat, and on one occasion, we had a small dead heifer trapped in the reed beds, not fifty yards from here, but most of the items we come across are things like plastic sheeting. We do seem to get more than our fair share of underwear, which makes me wonder what goes on along the river bank. Bodies do get caught up, like that one downriver near Newport. I suppose you were wondering if that Carter guy might turn up here. If he had made an appearance, we would have known by now as the smell would, quite literally, have been a dead giveaway, if you'll excuse the pun."

"I must admit that it had crossed my mind. We still have no idea what happened to him, and a lot of people in the village want to get the whole thing sorted."

"PC Daft Danny won't be a lot of help."

"You know our local bobby then?"

"Daft Danny has a reputation known by all people within a twenty-mile radius of here. He turned up at the cabin sometime just after Carter disappeared. He had convinced himself that someone could have hidden the body in the pond on the nature reserve, and he was talking about getting 'his' divers to come and search. I pointed out to one of the real police officers who turned up later that most of the pond, while it covers an extensive area, is less than two feet deep. A team of officers in full diving gear would have looked pretty

179

stupid wading around in a few inches of water. I did point out to the young coppers who turned up that the only possible place a body could have become caught up was in the extensive weed beds along the margins of the water.

"Some of the masses of vegetation were clogging up the water in places and had even started to work their way into the reed beds. I happened to comment that the guys might have to clear the weeds to see if the missing Mr Carter was concealed underneath. Bless 'em. The team raked out all the excessive weeds, but they didn't find a corpse. I knew that there wasn't enough space under the weeds to conceal a body, but the team were keen to be thorough. After two days, they had raked out mountains of the vegetation and left it in great piles along the edges of the pond. They were disappointed that their efforts had achieved nothing, but they were wrong. While the search for the body had been fruitless, the police team had made a very effective job of removing some non-native plants from the water. Those strapping young lads achieved in two days what would have taken me two weeks. Danny was disappointed, but 'his' search team were stood down."

"Yes, fate doesn't deal us many quite like Daft Danny in our lifetime, for which we should be eternally grateful."

"He means well and is diligent in his ineptitude. He started checking out those postcards in the post office window. You know, the ones about lost cats and the like. He would record them on his mobile and then pester the locals as to whether anyone had seen the lost pets. A well-intentioned plan but not the best use of police time. He wanted to put the pictures of the missing moggies up in the police station, but his superiors were less than impressed by his commitment to animal welfare. He means well, but he's just terminally useless."

The rest of the day was largely taken up with ensuring that an order was put in for some of the special equipment that Steve would need for his fieldwork on the nature reserve. This included waterproof clothing, waders and wellingtons. Bert then outlined some of the particular issues that it was necessary to look out for. Monitoring the water quality seemed an obvious task that needed to be carried out, but Bert also stressed the need to keep a note of any of the non-native species that the university were also watching.

"You'd be surprised at the number of different species we see that have been introduced to our waters," explained Bert. "Some brainless individuals have been known to release their unwanted pets into the wild. They may think they are being kind to the animals, but the truth is that some of them quickly die, like the piranhas that were reportedly found near Doncaster. Other species fit in well to their new environment, so much so that they drive out the native species, and it upsets the important balance within the water. One of our main problems at the moment is the introduction and rapid spread of zebra mussels."

"Zebra mussels? Are you having me on?"

"Sadly, no. The little buggers are finding their way into our waters. They breed at a phenomenal rate and overrun the native species. The particular problem that they cause us is that they can attach themselves to very smooth surfaces, unlike our native species. This enables them to form colonies in some of the extensive pipework we need for moving water around. They can foul up water intake pipes, which leads to increased cleaning costs for the authority. Last year, our water board alone spent half a million pounds getting rid of some of them."

"That would explain why the interviewing panel seemed to be so impressed by the fact that I had studied shellfish at university. Perhaps they thought I might play some part in eradicating infestations such as with the zebra mussels. I don't know how they would have responded if I'd explained that my special study was with whelks and, in Britain, they don't live in freshwater like zebra mussels."

"Typical! The bosses think they've appointed some sort of 'Mussel Man' superhero when they're actually employing Whelk Boy," quipped Bert. "But, never mind, you undoubtedly know more about what's going on in our waterways than the average member of the board of managers. The nearest some of them ever get to water is when they add it to their whisky. When I need someone to help me as we're waddling about in freezing water in the rain, then give me Whelk Boy any day rather than a man in a smart suit."

"Thanks. I think!"

"It's not only the mussels we have to watch out for," continued Bert. "We also have a range of plants that we need to control. The few sprigs of water plants bought at aquatic centres look lovely in an aquarium, and they can thrive, but some owners find their tanks become overgrown, so they decide to 'beautify' their local canal or pond with the excess. The plants thrive and soon form a mass of vegetation that prevents sunlight from getting down into the water. In places, they create a thick green carpet that can stretch for hundreds of yards. They block up waterways, and in extreme cases, it can lead to flooding. Most of the problems we face are not due to malicious activity but rather to a lack of understanding that things we do can tamper with the balance of nature. Our job is as much about avoiding extra problems in the future as cleaning our current mess up."

"I must admit that I was a bit perplexed at first when I read some of the issues in my job description, but now I see that the water board are not just about cleaning up water and providing it to the public; they have a vested interest in ensuring that the whole water cycle is working well. I think I'm going to enjoy this job."

"I'll remind you of that when you are up to your elbows in freezing water on a December morning, unblocking a water outlet while the rain trickles down your neck inside your waterproof coat."

By late afternoon, it was obvious that Denise was not going to make it back to the cabin before they were due to lock up.

"It's no surprise that she hasn't made it," observed the older man. "She often gets called out to meetings. Sometimes, I don't see her for days, and I know that deep down she would much rather be here, getting her hands dirty, so to speak. She's quite an expert in identifying birds by their songs. I know most of them, but she seems to know so much more; she often knows what each of the calls mean. She doesn't want to be stuck to a desk, but she knew it would happen as soon as she went for promotion. It appears to me that so many people are promoted out of their comfort zone; an individual may be brilliant in their job but find themselves moved up to a position that demands a completely different skill base."

Having made arrangements to meet up the following day at the cabin, the two men set off down the track towards the bridge. At this point, Bert turned right and headed up the Callerthorpe road while Steve turned left and, skirting the church, he headed back to see Georgia.

CHAPTER FOURTEEN

Steve was pleased to get back to see Georgia, who was just finishing the last of the clearing-up within the shop.

"So, how did your day go?" she asked eagerly.

"It's been a full day, and I've learned quite a bit about the wetland area, but I don't feel as if I've done any hard work. No doubt the job will have its moments, but today was a bit like going on a school trip. Denise was called away, but her colleague Bert introduced me to some areas of the work. He's a bit of a case, and I'm never quite sure when he's having me on. I was just pulling a bit of litter from the pond, and he advised me to beware of killer shrimp. I told him that I wasn't born yesterday, but he went on to explain that they do exist. They aren't likely to savage the unwary pond-dipper, but they are a menace to many of our native pond life. Apparently, they can grow up to 30mm long, and they are voracious predators of native freshwater shrimps and other aquatic fauna. They become sexually mature at about eight weeks and lay up to a hundred and fifty eggs at a time. Bert showed me the bulletin board in the cabin, which illustrates some of the plants and animals that we are to look out for; it's quite amazing. He intersperses items of fact among what is obviously a stream of fantasy, but he's easy to get on with, and I think we will be able to work together well. He has already decided to give me my own title; Whelk Boy. How was your day?"

"Whelk Boy? How did he come up with that?"

"I mentioned that I studied them in my time at university, and he seemed to find it amusing. He appears to march to a different drum some of the time, but it's never boring being around him. It would be easy to see him as just some sort of bumbling handyman, but he's obviously a very intelligent guy and dedicated to his work."

"I don't know what sort of world you've got yourself into, but it sounds as if it will suit you, although I'm worried about you having to go out and risk having to face up to killer shrimp. My day has been rather mundane in comparison. The shop has been relatively quiet, which is nothing new for a Monday, but it gave Rita and me a chance to chat about what's happening in the village. As she is keen to point out, Rita is no gossip, but she likes to know what is going on. She informs me that Mike Colly is planning to sell his place and move in with Stan. It seems silly for them to have two separate places, and Mike's tiny flat would not be as accommodating as Stan's cottage. Apparently, he takes every opportunity in conversations to refer to Stan as his son. I don't know if Mike has done the official paternity test yet, but he's been in touch with the social services to outline his plans, and I'm sure that they will be delighted to see the two of them together."

"Any news of Mark and Celia's plans? It's their engagement party on Friday at the Trout, isn't it?"

"Rita hasn't heard of any comments within the village. I expect most people will be pleased that they are having their little celebration, but Rita seems to suggest that there are those who view it in a somewhat patronising way, as if the young couple are just playing at planning to get married. It's like the 'weddings' that we acted out in class at primary school with various class members playing all the roles of the wedding party."

"Don't remind me of that. I was the groom in one such mega-performance, and the bride was Samantha Johnson. When it came to the point when the vicar announced that I could kiss the bride, she decided to be more proactive and lunged at me, kissing me firmly on the lips for what seemed like an eternity. I'm sure it took hours for my blushes to wear off, but the assorted audience of parents found the whole thing hilarious. I think Samantha was all ready for the honeymoon, and I was only six. It took years for me to get over that trauma."

"You appeared to have got over the worst effects of that experience by the time you met me, as I recall."

"I only managed with your gentle guidance and support, darling. After knowing you for a few weeks, I actually began to cope with you kissing me, and in time, I became rather fond of the activity."

"As far as I can remember, you coped pretty well on the first night that you walked me home to my hall of residence at university; you obviously learned a lot from your Samantha Johnson in primary school."

"Please let me try and forget her, darling. She meant nothing to me."

"Well. As I was saying, there are some people in the village who are not treating the engagement party as a serious prelude to a future wedding. They think it's 'sweet' that the young couple want to have a party and to be considered as being engaged. Mark and his friends are generally well-liked, but some people don't want to contemplate the prospect of a marriage, wondering how the pair will cope with life together. It's forcing people to recognise that Mark and Celia want to be together. It's tempting to talk in terms of 'developmental levels', but they are young adults with the same emotional needs as any other couple might have. As I see it, they will need some support, but then, each of them would need such support wherever they went on to live. Living with each other will no doubt throw up problems as it does with anyone, but it's clear that they are very much in love, and that's the best start they could possibly have."

"I suspect that some people will be concerned about the nature of any physical interaction between Mark and Celia," added Steve. "There can be a misconception that people with any form of disability are not interested in sex, and they are steered away from it by well-wishing carers. Colin has made a point of discussing the issue with Mark, and I gather that Celia's parents have never shied away from giving her whatever information she wanted. Obviously, when they do get married, they may need some more detailed guidance but, in the end, they will have to work on all aspects of their marriage as any other couple would do. It's generally acknowledged that half the fun of such a relationship is in exploring what it all means. It's a bit of a departure into the unknown for all couples but, in my experience, it's a journey that is well worth taking."

"I'll second that," concurred Georgia.

During the rest of the week, Steve gradually got used to his new job. Denise managed to get along to the cabin for a couple of days before being called out to fulfil some diplomatic role, representing the water company at a variety of meetings, including one in London. She was most apologetic about the fact that she could not spend more time introducing Steve to the complexities of his new job. In the time she was on site, she worked through some of the paperwork with him and explained the complex relationships between the various agencies who worked together to protect the water cycle in the area. She discreetly covered some of the inter-departmental politics, warning him of potential areas of minor disagreement with certain individuals he would be working with. It was while she was outlining one such area of lack of harmony that she suddenly moved quickly to the window and picked up the field glasses which always stood on the windowsill.

"He's back on patrol again," she exclaimed.

"Who is?"

"The marsh harrier. He's down there over the reed beds, heading in the direction of the bridge," she exclaimed excitedly, passing the field glasses to Steve. He stood for a while, locating the bird through the glasses and then watching as it headed off upriver.

"That is an impressive sight," he announced, "I've seen them in pictures but had no idea that they were so big. Do you see them a lot?"

"They are making a bit of a comeback in this area but they are far from common. There's probably a pair of them nesting in the reed beds somewhere in the wetlands, but if we suspect that there is a nest site, we stay well away from it; harriers are notoriously sensitive to being disturbed, so we just let them get on with it. We suspect that we know the area they may be nesting in and leave well alone."

"It's magnificent, the way he just seems to skim the top of the reed beds with his wings in that shallow V-shape. I've never seen one before. Are they rare?"

"In 1971, there was only one recorded pair in the country, but now there are a few hundred pairs, and many of them are in this part of England. It's a success story, largely due to the reduction in the generalised use of DDT and by ensuring that their wetland habitat is available. I've seen them quite a few times. One day, I was crouching over examining some insect larvae in the water just inside the reed bed, and when I stood up, I saw a harrier within a few feet of me. He seemed to appear out of nowhere. He just flew in so low and so quietly that it took me by surprise. It was a memorable experience. It was a bit of a shock, and I nearly fell backwards into the water; I don't think I did much to enhance the bird's day either."

By the time Steve turned up to work on Friday, he felt he had some slight insight into what his role at the reserve would be, but he had no idea how long he was likely to be working there. Bert was already in the cabin, and the two men sat down with a cup of tea to go over the day's agenda.

"We've had a bit of an alarming report from one of the university teams," said Bert as he shuffled through a few pages of correspondence. "It says that one of their team has found evidence of an infestation of zebra mussels down at the west end of the Reserve. Their researcher found a few of the little buggers down there, so we have to assume that there will be more."

"So what's the plan?"

"I usually get my shotgun out and blast the little devils to smithereens, but the noise can tend to alarm the local bird populations, and it costs a fortune in cartridges."

Steve was only momentarily taken in by this reckless suggestion and quickly asked if there might be an alternative solution.

"We've tried dynamite, but once again, some of the local eco-warriors can get a bit touchy."

"Is there an alternative policy as to how to deal with them?" asked Steve in an attempt to drag Bert back into something nearer reality.

"The first thing is to remove as many of the mussels as possible, and then, if there are infestations near the pipework, we get the scientific wallahs to feed the colonies with capsules laced with a poison that doesn't harm the waterways. We used to have to chlorinate the pipes and then rinse them through; it could take weeks, during which time we couldn't draw off any water."

"So, how do you go about removing any obvious collection of the mussels?"

"I'm glad you asked that. It means getting in the water and collecting them in a net or picking them out by hand."

"That sounds laborious."

"That's why we get a specialist in."

"Someone from the university?"

"No. This looks like a job for Whelk Boy."

"Me?"

"You'll be properly garbed up for the job. You didn't think those waders we supplied you with were some kind of fashion accessory, did you?"

"Thanks for your show of confidence; so when do we start?"

"The sooner we start, the better. I'll sort out some collecting buckets, and once you've got kitted up, we'll get to the site and start clearing up."

"And what exactly is your role in this expedition, Bert?"

"I'll be your wingman. I'll stand on the bank and hold your safety rope."

"Safety rope? Why would I need that?"

"They're cunning little devils. Usually, there's no problem, but if there's a rogue mussel among them, he might try and encourage the others to surround you. That's when I would pull you out before you get mauled. In my day, I would get in there clad only in a loin cloth and with a dagger clenched between my teeth for self-protection. But now, well, it's Health and Safety gone mad."

"Thanks, Bert, I feel so much better now, knowing that I have your support."

The zebra mussel safari went relatively smoothly; while Steve groped around in two feet of cold water, Bert stood offering verbal encouragement from the bank and laughing heartily when Steve almost toppled into the water. Two large buckets were filled with the offending bivalves, and these were carried back to the cabin and set aside to be collected for safe disposal. Steve was relieved to get out of his waders and wash some of the pond water from his arms. Having filed a brief report on the morning's activities, Bert made cups of tea, and the pair sat down to their respective lunches.

"You looked to be really enjoying yourself out there this morning," suggested Bert. "I would love to have joined you; there's something about the thrill of the hunt as you endeavour to outwit the mussels while keeping half an eye out for any marauding killer shrimps. I used to love the adrenalin rush, but after my accident, I have to be very careful."

Steve resisted the temptation to ask the nature of the said accident, fearing that it would give his colleague another opportunity to wander off into that alternative reality that the old man often inhabited. However, Bert was determined to outline his previous misfortune.

"It was a cold winter's day back in '96," he recounted. "The wetlands were frozen over when a call came in to alert us to the fact that water was incapable of getting through some of the iced-up pipes. Pausing only to pick up my ice axe and to clip on my crampons, I headed out into the blizzard with no thought for my own safety. Ignoring Denise's pleas for me not to go, I quickly ascertained where the problem was and set about breaking up the ice with my trusty axe. After a few minutes, I had weakened the frozen surface but then fell through and ended up to my waist in frozen water. I could feel the killer shrimps gnawing at my waders, and it was only my superhuman strength that enabled me to claw my way onto the bank. I tell you, lad, I was traumatised, and I've never been able to take ice in my whisky to this day."

"I'm glad you didn't tell me that before I ventured into that aquatic jungle, Bert," declared Steve, "But this job seems to offer plenty of variety."

"Believe me, lad, if you continue to work for the company, you will no doubt find yourself engulfed in all the excitement of sitting at a desk one day. When that happens, and you sit shuffling reports and files, you will look back at these days fondly."

"It didn't feel like that, trying to locate the mussels in what seemed like freezing water, but I suspect that you are right, Bert. Pottering around here in these peaceful surroundings suits me, but if I want to make a career for myself and go for promotion, then I will probably be dragged into the world of administrivia like Denise has."

"Don't get maudlin about it, lad. You might find you can hold on to this lifestyle. There are always temptations; pressure to earn more money, particularly if you find yourself with extra family responsibilities."

"Georgia and I don't have any rigid plans, but we need to think about what we hope to do in the future. We are lucky to have the flat above the shop, but it wouldn't suit us if we had any children. We haven't any plans for starting a family, but things may change, and children can be a major drain on finances, so I have to keep my career options open. I only hope that I don't get tempted along the lines of just chasing after big wages like my father did. He works all the hours he can and spends a lot of time away. He justifies it by saying that he needs to support my mum and me, but in the end, he's working to bring in money for things that we don't really need. He's sitting there now with Mum in a house that is more than adequate for their needs; nice car on the drive, big-screen TV and a healthy bank balance. They could afford to go on expensive holidays except that Dad is always working and he has no time for hobbies or socialising."

"It's a seductive path to be drawn along," agreed Bert. "Gina and I have settled for just being happy. We've had our wild times in our younger years and were tempted to make our fortunes in a variety of ways, but we weren't too disappointed when the money didn't roll in. We thought that panning for gold might pay off, but Gina is not keen on travelling these days, and it turned out that there wasn't a fortune to be made on the banks of the river Welland in Market Harborough. We set up camp, but after a couple of weeks, it was obvious that there was no gold to be had. This probably explains the lack of any other prospectors on the banks of the river, which had surprised us initially as it was so convenient for picking up provisions from Sainsbury's."

"Yes, it's strange that the banks weren't packed with great throngs of treasure seekers, all eager to share in the local bonanza."

"Perhaps we should have stuck at it, but the hours of constantly crouching at the riverbank played hell with the old injury Gina sustained during the shooting of *Predator*, so we reluctantly had to give it up."

After lunch, Steve was getting his weekly report sheet up to date when he received a call from Denise. Once again, she was apologetic for not having been able to spend more time with him during his first week but expressed her confidence in his ability to work alongside Bert. She reassured him that if he did need any guidance in the first few weeks, then she would be available on the phone. The call was cut short by her announcing that she had to go and sort out some issue. This left Steve wondering just how she managed to keep on top of the various projects that she appeared to be involved in, and he made a silent pledge to himself that he would never let himself be dragged into the upper echelons of management and allow himself to be run ragged by the constant demands on his time. Only time and domestic pressures would show if he would be able to keep this promise to himself.

It had been a very heavy day, but Steve had an inexplicable feeling of contentment as he walked home. He had finished his first week in his first 'real' job. He thought through his situation to establish just why he felt so happy. He quickly summed up his position. It was a lovely evening, and he had the prospect of time at the pub for the engagement party and then a weekend with Georgia. At the shop, he rushed up to kiss Georgia, but it was obvious that she was not keen.

"What's that smell?" she asked, and the disdain in her voice suggested that it was not an aroma that she was too enamoured with.

"Oh! That's probably the smell of the pond water. I had my waders on, but I managed to get my sleeves a bit damp hunting for zebra mussels. I guess I am a bit whiffy."

"You're right on that one. It smells a bit like a laundry basket full of damp clothes that have been left for a week or so. Go and get a shower before you come anywhere near me, and put your shirt in the bowl to soak."

"Don't I even get a kiss?" he pleaded.

"OK then," she said, giving him a perfunctory peck on the cheek.

"Is that it?" he exclaimed. "I spend a week toiling away in the wetlands, and all I get is the kind of kiss that a maiden aunt might give me."

"That's as much passion as you'll get from me until you've had a shower."

"So it's shower then passion?"

"Very limited passion; we've got the party at the pub this evening, and I want to take advantage of the excuse to get dressed up. It's just not your day, is it, sweetie?"

As there was no knowing what sort of buffet would be available at the pub, the couple decided to have sandwiches before they set out, with the option of having a light supper later if they felt they needed to when they got home. After his shower, and smelling appreciably better, Steve put on his old dressing gown and joined Georgia at the table.

"And now, am I irresistible?" he greeted her.

"Certainly more bearable, but get on with your sandwich; we've got to be at the Trout by half past seven, and we've both got to get dressed."

"Spoilsport!"

"To change the subject, if only to improve our chances of getting to the pub on time, Rita had some interesting news today."

"So what has she found out now? For a woman who claims not to like gossip, she appears to know everything that's going on."

"Rita was chatting in the post office with Mrs Holland and our postman, Barry."

"Barry, the guy who knows more about what's going on in our village than any official secret service organisation would claim to know?" he queried.

"The same. He was telling Rita that there have been some strange goings-on down at the caravan park where Brad Carter has a place. Mr Evans, the site owner, found a couple of guys checking over Brad's truck yesterday. He went over to see what was going on. The two men were in what Mr Evans took to be police uniforms, but it turns out that they were county court bailiffs, and they had official documentation to say that they were there to repossess Brad's vehicle. Apparently, he hadn't been keeping up payments on it, and the courts had ordered that his possessions should be seized to go towards paying off some enormous debts that he had run up. It had taken a while to find where Brad was holed up. It seems that the unsavoury Mr Carter had some quite astronomical gambling debts, and the bailiffs were interested to know if he owned the caravan as well. Mr Evans was eager to point out that, while Carter claimed he was buying the caravan, he had neglected to keep up the payments. In the end, the bailiffs took a few minor items of negligible value from the caravan along with the truck and left."

"That man causes nothing but problems for everybody he comes into contact with," commented Steve.

"Apparently, according to the oracle that is Barry, Carter owes over a hundred and eighty thousand pounds in total to a number of individuals, including at least three different bookies and a loan shark. The bailiffs must have been the least of his problems. At least Mr Evans is glad to see the matter is closed as far as he's concerned. The truck is off the site, and he only lost a few hundred pounds after Brad didn't keep up payments on the caravan."

"I bet Carter would be delighted that he's no longer going to be bothered by his debts. Anyway, if you are determined not to take advantage of me in my skimpy dressing gown, perhaps we'd better be getting ready to go out."

"You make it almost impossible for me to resist you, but I fear you are right."

"Thank you, darling. Your response is brutal but honest."

CHAPTER FIFTEEN

There were already quite a few people at the pub when Steve and Georgia arrived. Mark came straight over to meet them when they arrived. He was clutching Celia's hand while holding one of his special martinis in the other and obviously loving the festivities.

"Hello, my dear friends," he gushed. "My fiancée and I are very happy to see you here."

Celia smiled coyly and added her own greeting, "We are so pleased to see you at our party."

As usual, Celia had little time to say anything further as Mark went on to describe the plans for the evening and, more importantly, what food was available on the buffet. Monica had set out a very enticing display of sandwiches and various quiches and chicken pieces. She had also arranged a number of balloons and paper garlands to decorate the corner of the room that had been set out for the party. Mark, quite unnecessarily, pointed out the details of what was in the sandwiches and gave his personal ratings of each of them. His enthusiasm was infectious, but Steve and Georgia were relieved when other guests arrived, and Mark, with Celia in tow, went to treat them to his effusive greetings.

Colin took the opportunity to approach Steve and Georgia to greet them and introduce them to Celia's parents, Sandy and Margaret.

"The pub has put on a lovely spread for them," commented Margaret. "Celia has been talking about nothing else except the party since Mark proposed. I've never seen her quite so happy, and she has even started to talk about the wedding."

"She was a bit disappointed that her brother Josh couldn't make it this evening, but he says that he will make it to the wedding. He still has reservations about his big sister getting married. He's always been very protective, but I think he's starting to realise that she deserves a life of her own. He's still not entirely happy, but he's beginning to see things from her perspective, so we live in hope," commented Sandy.

"For the moment, we are just pleased to see her so happy," added Margaret, "and we'll just have to see how things progress. I think that Josh half expects Celia to change her mind about the wedding, but I rather think that they are set on the idea of getting married. There's been no talk of a wedding date, but both of them are keen to have a church wedding and a full reception, so we'd better start saving up."

"It's good to see so many people managed to get here this evening," observed Colin. "Particularly some of their friends from the day centre."

The sound of a fork tapping on a wine glass indicated that Mark was about to make a speech, and when the general chatter in the room had subsided, he stepped forward, still holding Celia's hand.

"My fiancée and I…" There was a pause while he suppressed an embarrassed giggle. "We are very pleased and happy to see so many of our friends at our party. Thanks to our parents for putting on this buffet. Please have a good time."

The announcement had the dual benefit of being brief and not including any jokes. Steve and Georgia wandered over to congratulate Mark on his speech.

"Very nice announcement, Mark. We have bought you a voucher to spend when you set up your new home."

"That is very kind; we shall buy something exquisite for our new home."

"Thank you very much," added Celia, still clinging to Mark's hand.

"It's our pleasure," added Georgia. "It was a lovely speech, Mark, and there weren't any jokes at all."

"Celia said no jokes today; it's very serious."

"No jokes," repeated Celia with an uncharacteristic firmness in her voice.

"No jokes today," confirmed Mark with a shrug of his shoulders, and the couple wandered off to meet other guests.

"Once again, I get the distinct impression that Celia is not the mousey little doormat that people might assume her to be. There's real hope for that relationship," commented Steve.

It was hardly surprising that the topic of Brad Carter's pickup and caravan were discussed at various times throughout the evening, and interest was further fuelled by the arrival of Danny Bright. He was thankfully not in police uniform but seemed keen to appear strangely officious, and when he made any contribution to conversations, it was almost as if he was giving evidence in court. After a few beers, he became slightly more relaxed but still wanted people to recognise his imagined authority.

"I've been trying to show my fellow officers that there is a disturbing possibility that the whereabouts of Mr Brad Carter have to be re-investigated," propounded the would-be detective. Aware that his comment had sparked some interest in the other party-goers, the local sleuth went on to expand his latest theory.

"It has come to light during the course of my investigations that our Mr Carter owed a lot of money, including to some pretty shady characters. His debts, and particularly those he owed to some rather nasty people, would have given him ample reason to want to disappear. It appears that his vehicle was not paid for, and he still owes money for the caravan he was living in, so he had no assets and massive debts. It is, therefore, I contest, highly likely that the aforementioned Mr Carter staged his own disappearance. Extensive investigations known as 'proof of life' measures have failed to find any evidence of his existence. We checked in all the usual ways; passport use, credit cards, and utility bills, but it's as if he just vanished from the face of the earth. If he wanted to engineer his own disappearance, then he's made a good job of it. I have to admit that even I, with my police training, was taken in."

There were comments to the effect of, "No! Not you, Danny," but the sarcasm was completely lost on him.

"I am currently exploring my new hypothesis with my colleagues. I have to admit that I was wrong about someone murdering Carter, but I'm not infallible."

Once again, there were exclamations of feigned disbelief, and the group who had been treated to Danny's latest interpretation as to the whereabouts of Carter, dispersed.

"I hate to admit it," declared Steve, "but there could be some sense in what Danny said, except that I don't believe that it's entirely his idea. As soon as the police found out about the debts and the fact that Carter was being sought by particular individuals, then the possibility of him wanting to disappear had to be considered."

"It does seem possible that Brad's offensive antics in the village were a charade to build up the idea that one or other of the offended villagers might have decided to top him and dump him in the river. You'll remember how, at the time, there was an extensive list of people who might appear to have had a reason to kill him, including yourself," surmised Georgia.

"Thanks for reminding me. I guess that the limited evidence about Carter's disappearance would have been easy to set up; a bit of blood on the parapet of the bridge and a whisky bottle conveniently found near the gorged river, when it might just as well have landed in the river and been lost. All he needed to do was to plant the evidence and then disappear. Perhaps he had some accomplice prepared to help him escape the area. Even someone like Brad would probably have had an accomplice who was prepared to help in his getaway for a price. The fact is that many people were more than willing to accept the idea that he'd gone over the bridge into the water. As the river was conveniently swollen, it was not a complete surprise that, even after all this time, nobody turned up, so it was quite possible that Carter had been swept away."

"Well, let's not let Carter spoil our evening. Party-on!" exhorted Gloria.

The engaged couple, and especially Mark, appeared to enjoy the celebrations, and he took particular delight in encouraging the guests to look at the engagement ring that Celia was wearing. At one point in the evening, Colin came over to chat to Steve and Georgia at their table, and they expressed their feeling that the party was going very well.

"I must admit that I had reservations about the prospect of Mark getting married," admitted Colin. "But now I've seen them together like this, I'm convinced that it's the right thing to do. I guess that a lot of parents feel apprehensive about letting their children go, and Mark's special needs certainly didn't make it any easier for me. Sandy and Margaret were also worried about letting go of Celia. It's hard to accept that your children could get by without you or that someone else might be able to take over from you when you know your child better than anyone else possibly could."

"You and Jackie obviously did a good job of bringing up Mark," added Georgia. "He's a fine young man, and the fact that he can even consider getting married is a testament to you both."

"Thank you, love, but as parents you never feel you've done enough. We'll just have to give them as much help as we can and then step back to let them get on with their lives. When all's said and done, at my age, I am increasingly aware that I'm not going to live forever, so Mark has to learn to get by without me. In a way, it was a bit more complicated for Celia's parents as they are relatively young and might reasonably expect to be around for a good few years to look after her. In that respect, I feel they have been a lot braver than me."

"How did Mark's social worker respond to the announcement that he was planning to get married?" asked Steve.

"She was very supportive and is looking into the possibility of finding supervised accommodation for Celia and Mark. There is a variety of schemes, but we would ideally want a placement that is not too far from here. We will just have to see what becomes available. Fortunately, Mark and Celia are not rushing to get married; they just both seem delighted to have made a statement by getting engaged."

At this point, Mark came over to join the conversation. For the first time that evening, he had released Celia and left her to show her admiring friends the engagement ring. Mark looked back at her and smiled broadly.

"She is beautiful. My fiancée. I have a smashing joke for you."

"I thought that Celia said we weren't having any jokes this evening," suggested Georgia.

"Just one really smashing joke for olden time's sake. Why do fish live in salt water?" Without giving his audience time to answer, he added, "Because pepper makes them sneeze."

"I think you'd better get back to Celia before she finds out you've been telling jokes," suggested Colin before turning to Georgia and Steve and apologising for the poor quality of the illicit jest.

"It wouldn't be an evening with Mark without his 'smashing' jokes," added Steve.

Their conversation was brought to a close by a commotion at one of the tables where there were signs of some sort of obvious celebration. Monica, who had been collecting at the said table, came over to collect some items from Steve and Georgia's table.

"Well, that's put paid to one of the least well-kept secrets in the village," announced Monica as she routinely wiped the table with a damp cloth.

"What's that?" asked Steve innocently.

"Barry has just proposed to Hannah Cordwell, and surprise surprise, she's accepted. Everyone knew that they had been seeing each other for months, but now it's official."

"I didn't know about that," confessed Georgia.

"Oh yes," declared the informed barmaid. "Whenever he went to the post office to collect the mail for his round, he always dropped in to see Hannah at the shop next door, and they were obviously 'good friends' as the celebrities always claim. Whenever young Karen came over to do a shift at the pub, she would recount what she'd observed while working at the shop."

"Well, good for Barry," exclaimed Colin. "He's taken one for the team. The men of the village will be glad to see that someone has fulfilled her romantic needs. We can all walk the streets safely at night now that Barry has taken responsibility; let's hope that he can keep her under control." With this parting comment, Colin wandered over to rejoin Mark's group.

"That's quite a turn-up!" observed Steve. "We come to one engagement party, and another engagement is announced. Perhaps it's contagious? We should go before we catch it."

"I can think of worse things than being engaged to you, Steve."

"Really?" he said, warming to this apparent sign of affection.

"Oh yes. Being trapped in a coffin full of spiders, lion taming, and contracting bubonic plague are all marginally worse than getting engaged to you."

"You really must control your rampant romantic spirit, darling."

"That's a shame because I was just about to suggest that we left, and I could get you home and encourage you to slip into something more comfortable."

"I would try and play hard to get, but it's just not my style, so let's just make our excuses and leave."

Halfway along the path back to their flat, Steve stopped and gave Georgia a lengthy kiss.

"Getting married isn't such a bad idea, you know, darling," he confessed. "We ought to at least give it some serious thought."

"Perhaps, but not after a rather convivial evening with a not inconsiderable amount of wine."

"I wasn't thinking of myself. I was more concerned about the considerable amount of money your mum would make from the sale of flowers for the wedding."

"You're so considerate but perhaps not too strong on your romantic timing. Now, perhaps I can get you home and help you make up for your less-than-amorous overtures?"

"I do love it when you're masterful," he declared as he smiled gently at her and took her hand.

CHAPTER SIXTEEN

The following day offered up a bright early autumn morning, but Steve and Georgia resented the intrusion of the sun into their room. They were not in any hurry to get up. It being a Saturday, Steve was enjoying a day off, and Georgia's mum had made plans for Rita to cover the work in the shop. As the couple lay in bed, they eventually heard the sound of Rita downstairs, busying herself with the routines of opening the shop. She didn't turn up until nearly nine o'clock, which, while it was hardly the crack of dawn, was a relatively early time for Georgia and Steve to be awakened on a day off.

"It's very good of Mum to let us stay here and to give me a job for a while, but I do wish we had a place of our own rather than being tied to the shop."

"It shouldn't be long now that I'm working, and you will probably not have to wait long before you find a 'proper' job. Then we can start making plans for the future. I agree with you that it would be wonderful to have a place of our own. Anyway, I suppose we ought to be thinking about making some breakfast rather than lying about in bed all day."

"Well! I never thought I'd ever hear you say that."

"I guess I'm just growing up at last," he declared before turning to her and adding, "Perhaps I won't grow up just yet."

It was after a late breakfast that the young couple sat with their cups of tea, making plans for their day off.

"Why don't we just chill out here all day?" suggested Steve.

"Not on your life. I spend almost my entire life here. I live here and work here, so staying in on a day off holds little appeal for me; so what is your Plan B?"

"As long as I'm with you, I'm happy," he declared, in an attempt to cover up what he knew had been an insensitive suggestion. "It's a lovely day, so why don't we walk down to the nature reserve, and you can see where I spend my day toiling to give the good people of the county clean water? I've got the key to the cabin, so we could drop in for a cup of tea and watch the birds on the wetlands for an hour or so."

"After our heavy partying last night, we could both do with some fresh air. I can make some sandwiches, and we could have a picnic."

"If it's going to be a picnic, then we should take the bottle of sparkling wine we've been saving in the fridge, and we can celebrate."

"I have no objection to that, but we don't have anything to celebrate."

"On the contrary, darling. After watching Mark and Celia together at their party last night, I was reminded again just how lucky I am to be with you. People may strive to acquire all sorts of stuff, but if they have no one to share their lives with, then they have very little. We are together, and that's more than enough reason to celebrate."

She kissed him gently and just said, "Thank you," before adding, "I'll get the wine."

The morning sun, whose appearance earlier had been resented by the young couple, now added a gentle autumnal warmth as they headed towards the bridge. Steve had a small rucksack containing a hastily assembled picnic, two glasses carefully wrapped in a small towel and the cherished bottle of wine. The latter had been set aside for an unspecified special event, but Steve could think of nothing more special than celebrating their good fortune at being together and being in love.

They resisted the temptation to take the small detour through the churchyard and pressed on over the bridge before turning right down the track towards the cabin. As they walked, Celia grasped Steve's arm with hers, and feigning mild terror, she asked, "Are we safe down here? What if we are ambushed by zebra mussels or killer shrimps? Will you protect me?"

"Don't worry your pretty little head, my sweet. In these parts, I'm not just Whelk Boy, I'm also the famous Shrimp Whisperer. The little varmints respect my authority. The zebra mussels can be a bit of a problem, but we can outrun them and hole up in the cabin."

Georgia smiled and released her grip on his arm. The couple walked in silence, experiencing the calming influence of the gentle sound of the wind rustling the reed beds. When they arrived at the clearing by the lake, Steve unlocked the door of the cabin, and they entered. He carefully put his rucksack on the small table, and they stood for a while looking out of the panoramic windows. It was a while before Georgia broke the silence.

"Doesn't anyone use this place at weekends?"

"It's the water company's unit, but various study groups can use it. It's in our interests to have as many people as possible monitoring the water quality in the area, so at least two university groups run research projects in the wetlands, and the local nature conservatory group can access the building at times. If there is some kind of urgent treatment needed to the water, then we can send in an emergency team who can be based here, sometimes at the weekends."

"You seem to have picked up a lot in your short time here."

"I'm starting to pick things up, but, as with all environmental issues, it can be very complicated. I'm only just beginning to get a vague idea of what's going on, but Bert and Denise are a big help."

"You obviously found something that you enjoy. It must be lovely to work in this environment."

"I must admit that I only considered this job in desperation because we needed to get some money in, but you're right; I really do enjoy it. It's not all sitting around admiring the scenery like this, but I still feel so lucky to be here. Even when we are busy, we can catch a glimpse of all sorts of creatures, like Harry, Stan's marsh harrier that I told you I had seen patrolling looking for his dinner. Speaking of dinner, I'm starving, so let's break out the picnic and give that wine an airing."

Georgia carefully arranged a variety of sandwiches and some small muffins on the table while Steve ceremoniously opened the wine and poured some for each of them.

"The pop of opening a bottle of sparkling wine always seems to evoke a party feeling, something special," commented Georgia as she took the glass she had been offered.

"A toast!" he declared. "To us and to love,"

"To us and to love," she repeated. "And now we should set about some of this food. I think I may have overdone the quantities again."

After a filling meal and finishing the wine, Georgia packed the empty bottle and the remains of their meal back in Steve's rucksack. Having made sure the cabin was locked, the couple set off on their walk home. They walked over the bridge hand-in-hand and then decided to cut through the churchyard. They still enjoyed spending time on 'their' bench by the church, and they were both looking forward to a few quiet moments. Rita would probably be starting to think about closing up the shop, and the young couple wanted a little more time on their own without being drawn into any conversation about the local gossip with her.

Because of this desire for a bit of solitude, they were just a little disappointed to see Stan and his dad sitting on one of the longer benches by the church, but they wandered over to chat with them.

"Been out for a walk?" enquired Mike.

"I've just been showing Georgia the place where I work; we both just fancied a walk, and the reserve is so peaceful."

"Yes, it's fascinating to see some of the birds down there," added Georgia.

"Stan and I felt that we needed a bit of fresh air and quiet after the party last night. It all got rather frantic later on after you'd left. Barry and Hannah Cordwell ended up dancing together, and Mark persuaded Celia to join in. It was quite touching to see the couples sharing their engagement evening."

"I'm sorry we missed it," said Steve, "but Georgia wasn't feeling too well."

Georgia was obviously a little surprised to hear of this newly diagnosed malady but resisted the temptation to explain that they'd had a quite different reason for leaving the festivities early.

"It was a good party," added Stan, who wished to contribute something to the conversation.

"It was a pity that Daft Danny insisted upon showing his less than comprehensive knowledge of the local police theory that Carter might have faked his own death to escape his creditors," commented Mike.

"Yes. I don't think people wanted reminding of him," agreed Georgia. "It was all a rather unpleasant experience. It was awful when Danny originally spread the suggestion that Martha had been murdered, and people started to wonder who had done it. The needless and unfounded rumours that he spread caused a ripple of unease in the village. His choice of prime suspect was ridiculous, as we know," she said while glancing surreptitiously towards Stan, who was blissfully unaware of her reference to him.

"Later, when he was convinced that Carter had been murdered, it further unsettled some of the locals, even if it was only a wish to know who the culprit was so they could thank them," added Steve, before suggesting, "That's enough talk of Carter. I've just remembered that we have the remains of our picnic in my bag. Do you think your friends might like to share it, Stan?"

"Thank you, Steve. They like surprises," replied Stan as he glanced at the contents of the rucksack.

"I'm afraid that I overestimated the amount of food we might eat," explained Georgia. "But I'm sure your friends can help us out."

Stan carefully broke the remains of the sandwiches and the muffins into small pieces before throwing them down, some feet from the bench. He explained that he had to ensure the food was in small pieces, or some of the larger birds would take a large chunk and fly off immediately. Steve was conscious of the fact that the four of them might put the birds off. It was a tight squeeze on the bench, but the group waited patiently and refrained from making any noise. Steve was surprised that it only took a few minutes for Paddy to descend and start picking out some of the choicest scraps of meat from the sandwiches. He had the feast to himself for a while, but eventually some smaller birds joined in the relocated picnic, and then a few rooks joined the party. The sparrows appeared to have no fear of the rooks that dwarfed them, hopping around between the big birds with relative impunity and picking up the small crumbs. Stan sat and watched with a smile on his face, but he didn't reserve any special treat to entice Paddy to come closer because he knew the bird would be wary of such a big audience.

Within a few minutes, the feast had been consumed, and the birds flew off, leaving a neatly cleared area. For a while, the occupants of the bench sat in silence as if in a reverence induced by the very tranquillity of the surroundings.

"The village seems so much more settled since Carter disappeared," mused Mike as he stared out in the general direction of the Trout. "And I can't think of anybody who would want to see him come back."

"He can't come back," said Stan, looking in the direction of Martha Turner's grave, before adding, "Gran wouldn't let him come back."

Mike smiled gently at this apparently misplaced faith that Stan still retained in his gran's ability to protect him. As they sat there that evening, it was easy to assume that there was some benign force causing an air of serenity to descend on the area. The locals had gone through a lot over the last few months, and it was as if the village was breathing a sigh of welcome relief.

"I certainly wouldn't want to see Carter's face in the village again," said Steve.

"He won't come back," declared Stan with uncharacteristic forcefulness.

"I'm sure your gran wouldn't want him to come back, son, but there's not a lot she can do about it now."

"He can't come back," repeated Stan. By this time, he was almost shouting, and this was something that nobody could remember him having done in his time in the village since his accident.

"It's OK, Stan," Georgia consoled him. "You're right; we shan't be seeing any more of that horrible man."

By this point, Stan had managed to work himself up into a state, and Mike realised that something was upsetting his son, so he attempted to find out what was at the bottom of this anxiety.

"It's alright, lad. He's gone now. It's all over."

"It wasn't Harry's fault," blurted out Stan's response.

Georgia, Steve and the older man looked at each other quizzically, but it was quite obvious that Stan was very concerned for his friend, the marsh harrier.

"I'm sure that Harry didn't do anything wrong," remarked Stan. "What makes you think he did?"

"The nasty man was on the bridge. It wasn't Harry's fault. They can't kill Harry."

Stan's small audience was further confused by this latest statement and looked at each other with a shared lack of understanding. In his agitated state, Stan tried to explain his thinking.

"When the dog bit the man, the news said the dog was killed. Wasn't the dog's fault. If animals hurt people, the animal is killed. Not fair. Harry was just being Harry."

"That was just a story on the news, Stan. You're not saying Harry attacked someone, are you?"

"No!" said Stan forcefully. "Harry was just looking for his dinner."

It was difficult to make any sense of what Stan was saying, so his father suggested he should calmly start the story from the beginning.

"I was getting my spade from my shed when I saw the man on the bridge. He was wobbly, and he fell over. Didn't get up, sitting on the floor, so I got my green box out of the shed. When I got to the gate, I saw him get up. Harry was just flying over, and the man was surprised. He was angry and tried to shake his bottle at Harry. Harry was fast and got away, but the man fell over again, and this time he just stayed on the floor, so I went down to the bridge with my green box to help."

"And how was the man, son?" asked Mike gently.

"Banged his head, nasty cut. He didn't move for a long time, so I carried him up to my shed. I put him in the chair and wiped his head with a wet cloth, but he didn't move. I felt for his pulse, like they do on the TV. I wasn't sure what I was feeling, but he didn't look like he was breathing."

"So what did you do then, son?"

"I kept an eye on him to see if he would get better, but he wasn't moving at all. Should have done 999 like on the TV, but I didn't want Harry to get blamed. It wasn't Harry's fault."

Stan was becoming obviously more and more agitated at the thought of his friend having injured Brad Carter, so Georgia attempted to reassure him.

"It wasn't Harry's fault, Stan. Nobody's going to hurt him. Carter shouldn't have tried to hurt him. It was an accident."

As the group sat together on the bench listening to Stan's unfolding story, there was a natural curiosity to find out what he had done with Carter but an understandable reluctance to press him for any details. Eventually, it was Mike who asked the inevitable question.

"And what did you do then, son?"

"I put him in the trunk. I wanted to see if he would be better the next day. I put the eiderdown over him to make him comfortable. Early in the morning, I looked again, but he hadn't moved, and he looked different. He wasn't going to get better."

"You didn't leave him there, did you?" asked Steve, fearing what might happen to a corpse left for some while in a chest in the shed.

"No."

"So what did you do, son?" pressed Mike.

"I buried him. I do burying."

"Where?" asked Steve.

"Here in the churchyard, so it was a proper place."

"Where exactly?" asked Georgia.

"Over there," answered Stan, gesturing in the direction of his gran's grave.

"Near your gran's grave?"

"No. He's in Gran's grave."

There was a lengthy silence as Stan's audience took in this latest piece of the mystery, but eventually it was Mike who had to ask exactly what Stan meant.

"You put Carter in with your gran?"

"No!" he answered firmly. "Gran wouldn't want that."

"So what do you mean, son?" asked Mike calmly.

"I had dug Gran's grave. It was all ready for her. I dug down a bit further to make a space for the man and then covered him up. Next day was Gran's funeral, and she was put in on top of the man's grave. Steve helped me fill in the grave before we went to the party at the pub."

"And no one saw you putting Carter in the grave?" asked Steve.

"I did it in the night before Gran's funeral. No one was around except some of my friends, and they won't tell anybody. It didn't take me long. I'm a good digger."

"And that would explain why your boots were all muddy when we met up on the morning of the funeral and the fact that you'd changed in your shed," reasoned Steve.

The group sat without saying anything for a while; Stan was apparently a bit relieved that he had been able to share his guilty secret, and his audience sat in a kind of numbed silence as they assimilated the information and the possible consequences of Stan's disclosure. It was Stan who eventually tried to come up with a solution.

"I'll have to tell Constable Bright what I did with the man. It wasn't Harry's fault. They won't hurt Harry, will they?"

"Honestly, Harry will be fine," Georgia consoled him. "But I don't think Danny Bright needs to be informed at the moment. We have to think this through. Why don't you go and make cups of tea for you and your dad? He was saying that he'd love a hot drink and perhaps some of your biscuits?"

Having effectively excluded Stan from the conversation for a while, Georgia outlined her immediate views on the situation.

"I guess that we should inform the authorities about what we've just heard, shouldn't we? But it doesn't seem right."

"Stan was only acting to protect his friend; he obviously thought that Harry could be put down for startling Carter on the bridge. A judge would only have to see Stan to realise that the lad thought he was doing his best," added Mike.

"One would hope so," interjected Steve. "But it could emerge that Carter was the individual that caused the catastrophic injuries to Stan, and it might be suggested that Stan got his revenge by attacking Carter on the bridge before disposing of the body in a grave that had been prepared in advance. It could be suggested that it had been premeditated."

"Nobody could possibly believe that of Stan," protested Georgia.

"Daft Danny Bright would be in his element and keen to show his legendary 'local knowledge'," replied Steve. "Remember how keen he was to inform the village that Andy Cordwell had run over Stan. He was then convinced that Stan had killed his gran and, to top it all, when Carter disappeared, he was intent on suggesting that Stan was a prime suspect."

"On that last point, Daft Danny was perilously close to being near the truth for once in his life," suggested Georgia.

"We have to consider what will happen when we tell the authorities," continued Mike. "They would start by having to dig up Martha's grave to confirm that she has a lodger in the basement. Stan will need to be prepared for that eventuality. For some bizarre reason, he loved the old woman, and he would be devastated to see her having to be exhumed and knowing it's because of what he did with Carter's body."

"There is another course of action open to us," mused Georgia before adding tentatively, "We could forget we ever heard anything about it."

There was a long silence as the trio mulled over the consequences of such inaction. It was Mike who first came up with his views.

"It wouldn't be easy to keep the whole episode a secret. Stan is a very honest person and might be tempted to tell someone else about it."

"You're right," agreed Steve. "But if we made it clear that we wanted to keep Harry out of all of this, despite the obvious fact that it has nothing to do with the bird, he is less likely to tell anyone. We could even tell him that he did the right thing by giving Carter a resting place in consecrated ground."

"We have to make it clear that he mustn't tell anyone about it," suggested Georgia.

"Naturally. But the fact is that if he did ever tell anyone, they probably wouldn't believe him and just assume he's confused," pointed out Steve.

"There is one little legal point that we ought to bear in mind. Technically, you would be guilty of assisting in the improper disposal of a corpse; you helped cover up the body," teased Georgia.

"I think we would all have legitimate reasons not to disclose what we have heard because none of us want the lad to be put through the turmoil of a police investigation. I know we ought to reveal we know, but how would it help? The legal system might be satisfied, but would justice be served? I wouldn't want to be at home with Stan watching him fret over the issue, and I definitely wouldn't tell anyone if we decided to keep a respectful silence."

"I can see no benefit from disclosing what we have heard," commented Georgia. "And, though I'm reluctant to speak for Steve, I'm sure that we agree on this."

"I certainly do, and we will make absolutely sure that we tell no one. It only takes the rumour mill to start up, and the whole village would know. I'm quite convinced that most of the villagers would be slow to criticise Stan for his action, and they'd be delighted to know that Carter will never return, but if word got around, then even the inept Danny Bright would detect what had been going on, and he wouldn't ignore it."

"So we agree to keep this matter among ourselves," said Mike. "This whole conversation never took place. I'll continue to reassure Stan that he did right but that we must keep it a secret to keep Harry out of it."

"And we'll make a point of never bringing up the subject of Carter's whereabouts with Stan."

It was at this point that Stan arrived with two cups of tea and a packet of biscuits.

"Thanks, son," said Mike, accepting his tea. "We've just been having a chat about your friend Harry. You're right; he didn't do anything wrong. You behaved very well when you buried Mr Carter in consecrated ground; it was the proper thing to do."

"I dig good graves."

"You certainly do, lad; you did a good job, and the man is at peace now."

"I said Gran wouldn't let him come back. Gran will look after him. Gran is good at looking after people."

"She's looking after him, just like she looked after you," added Georgia, conscious of the fact that this sentiment was open to various interpretations.

The group sat, squashed together on the church bench, each wrapped in their own thoughts as they took in the peaceful ambience of the early evening. The village was returning to its natural, untroubled state. In the grand scheme of things, Brad Carter had been merely an annoying disruption to the tranquillity of the place, but now he was gone, and while his whereabouts would continue to be a mystery for most, he would not be missed.

It was Mike who summed up the feelings of the group when he announced, "I know it may not be entirely legal, but I'm convinced that we are right to let sleeping grans lie."

ABOUT THE AUTHOR

Born in Hull in 1949, I went to Beverley Grammar School, where I directed far more of my energies to my social life and sport rather than academic pursuits. I drifted on to Sheffield to train to be a teacher because I was too young to know better. After 37 years, largely in special schools, I was able to take early retirement and reclaim my life. My career took me and my family to Grimsby, Hebden Bridge and Knaresborough before moving south. It is ironic that my wife, Lynne, took on a disproportionate amount of our domestic duties and parenting to allow me the time to set out on a series of academic studies to help me in a career for which she was much better suited. Along the way, we managed to produce three children, one of each. Sadly, Lynne, who was a very talented and dedicated teacher and mother, died last year after years of struggling with Alzheimer's. I remain an unrepentant romantic, currently living near Winchester.